VEBECCA FISCHER

Only a Deal

Copyright © 2023 by Vebecca Fischer

All rights reserved. No part of this publication may be reproduced, stored or transmitted in any form or by any means, electronic, mechanical, photocopying, recording, scanning, or otherwise without written permission from the publisher. It is illegal to copy this book, post it to a website, or distribute it by any other means without permission.

First edition

This book was professionally typeset on Reedsy.
Find out more at reedsy.com

To Jeff for reminding everyday that I need to write and finish this thing

Contents

1

Chapter 1

It had been two weeks, and there was still no change. Zo looked down at her twin, Ze, for the past two weeks, he'd been bedridden. He'd been sick before, but nothing like this. Every healer, magic or otherwise, had said the same thing. 'We've done all we could. He needs rest and time.'

That wasn't good enough for Zo. They'd been together their whole life, and it had always been them against the world. They'd made friends, traveled, and worked with them, but it was different. She'd never been in the world by herself. To see Ze so sick and weak like this hurt, and she had to do something.

Zo'thre, Zo to friends and her brother, was a small but built half-elf. After spending more time outside than in, she'd gained a constant tan that always made her a few shades darker than her brother. Her hair was a dark brown, almost black, and fit well with her other dark features.

She took a final look down at her brother and then got up from the chair she'd been planted in for the last two weeks. Ze'zein had always been pale even as a child but now he was almost ghost-like. His dark brown hair clung to his face and had been turned black by his constant sweating. Since Ze had become bedridden she had barely moved from his side. Their friends had been worried and tried to make her take shifts with them, she'd have none of it. If her brother needed something she wanted to be there for him.

The door opened as their friend Primalis came in she was holding some blankets to help change the sheets. Ze's constant sweating made them need to change the sheets almost every day.

"You're awake, I came in earlier but you were asleep. I didn't want to wake you. You needed the rest," Primalis said. She always spoke as if she didn't know if she was allowed to or if she was scared of offending or upsetting someone.

She was a half-elf with brown-reddish hair. She looked like she belonged more in the middle of a grassy meadow or wooded forest rather than on the edge of a bustling city where their house was.

Zo didn't have the heart to tell her she hadn't been sleeping. She'd slept little the last few weeks and knew she wasn't going to till Ze was better.

"Yeah, I needed the rest," She told Primalis with a slightly strained smile. She was grateful for her friends but nothing was helping. There was a silence that then fell over the room.

"Oh, I infused the sheets with healing herbs. I don't know if it'll help but it might. You know...," her words drifted off. She looked like she'd made a mistake talking and her eyes drifted toward Ze.

"I'll try almost anything at this point."

"Don't say that! You never know who's listening." Primalis was suddenly very worried. She looked around and seemed to let out a sigh of relief but was still on edge. She always seemed a little uneasy but this was a lot for even her.

"Why are you so jumpy there aren't any fae doors near here."

"That's right, you wouldn't have heard."

"Heard what Primalis?"

"A fae door opened at the north edge of the Nole Forest. I know it's a few days from here, but you know."

"Yeah, I know."

"I just thought you should be careful. You never know you know."

Zo nodded slightly and looked out the window towards the woods. From their small house on the edge of town, they were about an hour or two walk from the edge of the woods. To actually get through the woods and to the other side would take a day or two if you knew your way but it could easily take a week if you took a wrong turn or didn't know your way.

By herself, she could get there in a day if she was quick. A day away and if she was lucky she could talk to a fae. It'd be dangerous and most likely not worth it but it also could definitely be worth it. It could mean healing Ze, which was most definitely worth it to Zo.

Primalis was busy changing the sheets she was gentle with Ze. Making sure he was handled with care and whispered to him. Letting him know exactly what she was doing. If he could hear her or not was another story. Her fingers lingered on his cheek after she brushed some hair away. Zo made a mental note of it but would didn't bring it up. Once her brother was better she would talk to him about it. Primalis was a friend but getting close to people was dangerous. It just led to them getting hurt.

Zo knew if she told Primalis she'd try to stop her so she'd need to leave tonight and get there in the morning. It would be the fastest and easiest way. For now, she'd have to wait and plan. It wouldn't be too hard. A quick trip like this would need some careful planning. She didn't want to be gone for more than two days. But realistically she'd be gone for about three to four days. Even if she could go on little rest, she would need sleep. Currently, Zo was running on a few hours a day when her body made her sleep. It wasn't an ideal situation but it would have to do.

"I made some stew if you're hungry," Primalis said clutching the old sheets. "I could bring you up a bowl."

"That'd be nice. Thank you, Primalis," Zo told her. The herbs Primalis had infused the sheets with did smell nice. Even if it didn't help Ze get better, it was lovely. Primalis specializes in herbs and potions. She'd tried more than a few things to help Ze. Each time something didn't work, she looked more and more deflated. Zo didn't blame her. She hadn't been the only one to try and fail to get him better.

Primalis nodded and turned to leave. She then stopped pulling a rolled-up piece of paper from her pocket.

"Sallen and Wina sent word. They arrived at the Solar temple. Hopefully, they'll be able to get holy water and maybe some answers," She said, handing over the note.

Zo took the note with a nod. Primals gave her a small smile and then left to room.

Sallen was a gnome with the lightest brown hair Zo had ever seen that wasn't just blonde. He was loud and never stopped talking; it had always annoyed Zo, but now the house was too quiet without him here. Wina was a halfling who, on the other hand, had the darkest blonde hair without being brown that Zo had ever seen. She'd always been the voice of reason in their group but was also at a loss. Neither of them stood over four feet. Since no traditional healing magic had helped, she offered to talk to people at the Eastern Solar temple of Ish. It was the deity Wina followed and hoped she would be able to find something to help Ze there. Sallen had gone with her because he didn't want to stay twiddling his thumbs and feeling useless.

Even though Zo and Ze didn't follow Ish, Wina insisted it might help. As Zo had said, she was willing to try anything. She could also tell that her friends were just as worried as her. And wanted to do anything they could to help.

Letting out a sigh, Zo got up. She pulled the blankets around Ze a little tighter. The sun had begun to set and she needed to start getting ready if she was going to the north side of the Nole Forest.

"I'll be back soon. You better be better when I get back. I love you," Zo told her brother. Then kissed his forehead. They weren't ones to tell each other I love you. It was more of an implied thing. They weren't overly affectionate since neither was their father, who had taken to raising them solely at 10. But she didn't know what she was walking into or what she'd come back to. She needed to tell him and reassure him. But if she was being honest, it was more for herself than for him.

Making her way downstairs, she caught Primalis bringing her some stew.

"I thought it might be good to have a slight change of scenery. Mind if we eat together down here?" Zo asked her.

"No, not at all. Come, there's a fire in the kitchen," Primalis told her. She was surprised Zo had left Ze's side but was glad she was moving around.

They ate in relative quiet. Primalis tried to make a little bit of small talk, which would have usually annoyed Zo but comforted her tonight. The house had been way too quiet as of late. After eating, they cleaned up the kitchen. Zo did her best to feed Ze a little broth, but he could hardly manage any. Primalis started washing the sheets, which Zo helped with when she was done trying to feed Ze.

No matter how hard they tried, there was still an air of sadness over them. Usually, the house held seven people and was cramped but with just the two of them to fill the space, it felt empty and uninviting.

Zo told Primalis good night and made her way to her room. She lay down in her bed with no intention of falling asleep. Instead, she listened to Primalis move around the house.

She stayed in the kitchen for a little longer, probably working on another herbal remedy or position to try and help Ze. After a few hours, she moved upstairs to the bedrooms. Instead of going into her room Zo heard her go into Ze's. Then nothing. She'd most likely filled the chair Zo had taken up residence in the last few days.

Waiting a few more hours till the moon was high in the sky. Zo then quickly packed a bag. She grabbed her traveling cloak and wrote a simple note for Primalis. Saying she thought of something that might help and she'd be back in a few days. Please take care of Ze while she was gone.

She quietly walked through the house. Avoiding any and all squeaky floorboards. Passing by Ze's room, she saw Primalis asleep with her head resting on the foot of the bed. Her hand was stretched out, holding his. A slight pang of guilt and annoyance hit her. There definitely would be a talk with Ze when she got back. But this wasn't the time for that.

At the door, she grabbed her bow and arrows and her daggers. She let out a breath she'd been holding and then walked out of the house with only the moonlight to guide her.

2

Chapter 2

The walk to the edge of the Nole Forest wasn't bad at all. No one else was out at this time of night so Zo didn't have to worry about running into anyone. She also didn't have to worry about how fast or slow her companions could go. It was just on her. The only downside was she had to keep more of a watchful eye. Stealth wasn't something that could happen in a big group, but the group also meant safety.

The forest had been where she'd spent most of her childhood and teens. And it had been the place she'd retreated after Ze and her had left their father's house. Where Ze found solace in blending into the big crowds of cities. Zo always liked the wildness of the woods better. She felt at home there. Which was another reason she knew she'd be able to get to the northern edge of the forest quickly.

She knew she could go most of the night but would have to stop before she reached the northern edge. Her plan was to go far enough that Primalis or anyone else wouldn't be able to follow her. It shouldn't be too hard. Nothing against Primalis, but firstly she wasn't great at tracking, next her endurance was much lower than Zo's. There was another thing on Zo's side, stubbornness.

It wasn't that she held it as a point of pride. She knew that her stubbornness had made it so she and Ze got this far. And it had gotten them and her out of some pretty bad situations throughout the years. So she was going to use it to get them out of this bad situation too.

Traveling all night the first rays of light began to fill the forest floor. She'd traveled far enough and covered her tracks well enough that being followed was no longer an issue. Looking around, she found a tree with good enough branches and cover that she could sleep there for a few hours.

Even though she wasn't sure she'd be able to sleep she knew she needed to. Sleeping in the forest alone wasn't something she was unfamiliar with, but it had been a long time since she'd done it. Since her late teens, it had been her and Ze. Now she had a group of people she trusted. The lone girl in the forest wasn't something that she really had on her resume anymore.

It'd been years since the last time but the old habits and necessities of being in the woods alone came back to her quickly. It had been second nature years ago and only took an hour or two of being back to become second nature again.

Zo woke up to the sound of leaves rustling around her. Her first instinct was that she was under attack or an animal was in the area. Automatically reaching for her bow, she stopped herself. It was just the wind.

It was a calming breeze, and the rustling acted like a lullaby trying to keep her asleep. As calm and tranquil as the setting was, she quickly remembered why she was there. Making sure she had everything Zo hopped down from the tree and continued on. She needed to get to the northern edge today. The only thing she was worried about was the fae door.

Not the door itself, but it still being there. Fae were fickle creatures and no one knew how or why doors to the fae realm opened. They seemed random, but also not. Which was very fae. Some people said they were there for a reason. Their arrival and placement were a big plan by the fae. That's why you should never trust a fae you never knew what they were planning and they were always at least five or six steps ahead of you. There were others who said it was utterly random on all accounts and the fae had just adapted to it which was why you should never trust one because you never knew what they would do but neither did they. Everyone agreed though, never trust a fae. And here Zo was, walking willingly toward one to ask for help.

She knew enough about dealing with fae. That being said, she'd never dealt with one herself so all the knowledge she had was second-hand, rumors, pub talk, or old wives' tales. The closest she'd ever talked to anyone who'd actually dealt with the fae was a very drunk man in a pub. And it wasn't even him who had dealt with it. It was his sister's friend's cousin. Which wasn't the most hopeful or helpful information. But it was all she had.

All around her, the forest moved as animals and plants went about their business. There was no sign that only a few miles away was a fae door leading to a realm of chaos. The forest around her went about its day, not paying attention to the half-elf walking through. Zo completely admitted it was calming and pleasant to get out of the house. She hadn't left her brother's side since he fell ill. She was looking forward to when Ze was feeling better and they would be able to take a new job. To get out of the house together, like they always did.

Her, Ze, and their friends were technically adventurers but if they were being honest they'd take any job that paid decently. And more than a few that didn't when they needed the money.

The forest continued on, Zo made her way through it without much trouble. She knew how to avoid any animals that would cause her problems. Any people that were also walking through the forest were either easy to avoid or easily avoided her. Without any distractions, she made it to the northern edge in about two hours.

Now she just had to find the door. Primalis hadn't given her any details. And she had a feeling if she'd asked the other women would have become suspicious and would never have left her side.

The northern side of the Nole Forest was sparser than the rest of it. Mainly consisting of more samplings than larger older trees. That meant Zo wouldn't have to quote on quote dig for the door. It should be somewhat easy to find.

After a bit of walking, something caught her eye. She'd slowed to a steady pace that one might call leisurely in some other circumstance. Most of the way she'd alternated between a brisk jog or walk to not tire herself out but still make good time.

There was an almost golden arch in a small clearing. Zo had pictured a wooden door like the one in their house. But it made sense there wasn't just a wooden door in the middle of a forest some were. On the other hand, it was the fae so she didn't really know what to expect.

The arc was translucent and could have easily been missed especially in direct sunlight. The only way Zo saw it was because she was looking for something. From the right angle on the side, it gave off a sparkle-like strip of gold left in a field. The reflection of the sun was what caught her eye and drew her to it.

Standing in front of what she could only assume was the opening, Zo could see an almost exact replica of the clearing and surrounding forest on her side. When she went around to the other side it was as if the door didn't exist. She just saw the forest at the edge of the clearing.

Well, she'd found it and now she just needed to go through it. She'd done what she came to do find the door. Now she needed to go through and find a fae. Then she would need to make a deal with one. Heal her brother, that's all she wanted and that was what she would get. She just hoped the price wasn't too high.

Zo mustered up all her courage and walked through the arch. It was an odd feeling. She felt hot and cold at the same time. Her head tingled she wouldn't say it hurt, just tingled. Like she'd touched some of Primalis numbing jell but it was in her brain. It wasn't unpleasant just different.

Then she was in a clearing just like the one she'd been in, but things just seemed off. She couldn't put her finger on what seemed off. Things just did. As unsettling as it was, she'd have to worry about it later. This was no time to sightsee. She didn't know Ze's current condition or how much longer he could go on like this.

There was a tree line a little bit away from her surrounding the clearing. Just like the other side expert opposite. It was almost a mirrored reflection of the world she'd just come from.

With purpose, she walked into the field towards the tree line and tried to see if she could spot anyone. As far as she could see there was nothing. Walking a little away from the door she started to look around for tracks. But found nothing. Actually, she wasn't even leaving tracks. So tracking was entirely out of the question.

Not seeing anyone and there being no tracks. Zo was left with one option. She yelled into the clearing a very loud and confident, Hello? The clearing was quiet. An eerie quiet. That was what was off. There was no noise. No wind, no animals, no nature just being. The only noise she heard was her. The realization left her more unsettled than she'd like to admit.

After her call, she still didn't see anything. Now annoyed.

"Well, fucking a," Zo yelled at the tree line. She then spun on her heel not wanting to waste time. This landed her right into the chest of what she could only assume was a fae.

"There's no need for profanity," A deep voice said from above her. The person, fae? He was at least a good ten inches taller than her. Hands had come out and gripped her arms to help steady her when she'd run into him. It seemed to surprise him just as much as her, but he had recovered faster.

Zo jumped back and took in the man in front of her. He was slender but not wiry. When she had been pressed against him, she'd felt muscle but not bulk. He was pale but in no way seemed sickly even though he might even be paler than Ze currently. His hair was almost an unnatural white. As if he'd gotten it from trauma rather than age. He wore a long dark coat that she would expect to be more ornate but it was simple in nature. His face was obscured by a mask that was of an animal but Zo couldn't place the species currently. If she had to guess she at least knew it was a bird. An ora of grey mist around him made it look like he wasn't really there. Or he wasn't real.

She couldn't see his face but his head cocked to one side as if he was waiting for her to say something. The action made Zo think of a puppy waiting for you to give it a scrap of your food or wanted attention.

When she didn't answer, he took it as he would have to talk

first. He sounded a little disappointed at that, but it didn't seem to deter him from asking.

"So you were looking for me?"

3

Chapter 3

There was a brief silence till Zo found her voice again. She wasn't sure what she was expecting, but it wasn't this. He was unlike anything she'd seen before. For many people that would be enough for them to want to run or scream. But working as an adventurer and seeing new and unique things was not out of the ordinary.

"Well not you specifically, but a fae who was willing to make a deal," Zo told him. She tried to sound confident and not let her voice shake.

"I see no others here," He responded. Zo had to remind herself that to the fae, words were power. She would have to be careful with them.

"This is your door then?"

"They aren't our doors. We just use them and others have called them ours. I stumbled on it a while ago. And being a naturally curious person. I stayed to see what wonders would come through the door."

"Do you tell everyone this story, or am I just special? Or is it the sound of your voice that you like?"

The fae stopped. The mask made it hard to tell what he was thinking, but the best Zo could tell was he seemed more alert now. She wasn't sure if that was a good or bad thing. Only time would tell.

"You're an interesting one. I think I may like you," He said after he was done assessing

"Enough to help me?" Zo questioned.

"You have a problem?"

"My brother, my twin, is sick, I would like to have him healed."

"And you're here to make a deal for it?"

"If it's out of your power..."

Silence settled over the clearing. Zo was sure if she could see his face he'd have a look of annoyance. If she wasn't as observant she would not have noticed his shoulders drop slightly. She decided not to pick at it since Ze's life was on the line but made a mental note about it.

"In any case, I won't make a deal with someone whose face I can't see," Zo said, crossing her arms. It was not supposed to be a defensive motion, more of an adamant one. She didn't care if he was fae she wasn't going to make any deal with someone who she couldn't at least see some of their face. But she left out how much of their face for his interpretation.

"Many have made the mistake of asking to see my face," he told her, getting closer. Since the conversation had started, they'd kept a decent amount of distance from each other. Close enough to still hear one another but far enough not to be within reach. After the initial running into one another, Zo was happy to keep it this way.

"Why's that?" she questioned.

"Because then I could say no." She could hear the smile in his voice which she wasn't sure if it was a good thing or not.

He brought his hand up to his face and waved it across, grabbing at the mask. The mask then turned into the black mist that surrounded him.

"I've decided I do like you. Now you wanted your brother healed, no?"

She wasn't sure what she was expecting on the other side of the mask, but it wasn't this. The fae looked almost human but off somehow. His eyes were too blue to be natural for a human, but they weren't unnatural. His skin was pale almost to the point of being sickly, but he looked to be in peak health. His hair was white to the point that she'd never seen on anyone and only seen in very high-ranking monarchs. She knew no one got hair that color unless under extreme duress. In other circumstances, Zo would have called him handsome, but something just off about him was still unsettling.

"Fae don't do anything for free," Zo said, not elaborating on purpose. See what he wanted and not give up anything till he put down his price.

"True. How about this? A life for a life?"

Zo cocked an eyebrow at him. Waiting for him to elaborate. There was a slight smile when she didn't immediately respond to him.

"You're first born for your brother's full recovery."

"A little cliche, isn't it? My firstborn?"

"The classics are the classics for a reason now aren't they."

For a few moments, she thought about it. Putting on a little bit of a show for him. As if she was torn about giving up a future child.

"That sounds fair," Zo responded. She knew with fae it was everything that wasn't said that mattered. He just said to give him her firstborn, not that she had to. So she didn't have to have a child just if she ever did it would be forfeit to him.

He gave her an inquisitive glance and then made a slight humming noise.

"I think a three-year time limit would be fair as well. Don't you agree?"

"That sounds very fair." She kept her voice even but couldn't help but be impressed with him. She knew fae were smart, but she wondered if he was particularly smart. She would need to outwit him. But giving her a time limit meant she did, in fact, have to have a baby. But he did not say who the father had to be. She had complete control over that.

"If you are not able to give me your child in three years' time, then your brother will revert back to his current state. And may his fate be in the hands of the Gods."

Zo just nodded as he spoke. Not giving him anything. It seemed to either confuse or amuse him she wasn't sure which. His expression was hard to read.

"I take it we have an agreement?" He asked her when she didn't disagree.

"Within three years' time, I'll give you our child for my brother's full recovery. Yes, we have an agreement."

"Wonderful, your brother is fully healed and will be in the best health of his life. Just remember our deal."

"Yes, of course, when would you like to start?"

"Excuse me?"

"I said within three years I'd give you our child. Which means you're the father. So do you want to start trying now?" Zo asked as she started to undo the laces on her jacket.

The fae looked like this was the first time anyone had outwitted him or used his own words against him. Also, she could see a tinge of pink starting at the top of his ears. He was embarrassed.

He took in a deep breath and let it out before continuing with the conversation.

"I see, you did. Well..."

"You didn't want to start right away. Alright, when would be best for you?"

"Firstly, very well played. Second I will hold up my end of our bargain but not here in the middle of a clearing. Thirdly this means you're mine till this deal is complete. What is your name, elf?" He said the last thing with the undertone of a threat. Zo wasn't sure if it was to scare her or not, but it was definitely taking possession of her.

"Half-elf, and I want to know yours as well."

"Names have power."

"I know, but I would like to know the name of the father of my child. And we should keep this as fair as possible."

"True, I will also put my mark on you. So that others know you're mine and I can find you where ever you are. I need to protect to mother of my child, don't you agree."

Zo gave a nod in agreement. He then walked over to her and leaned towards her ear so only she could hear him.

"Quinton," he said barely above a whisper. If the clearing hadn't been, this quiet, she would have missed it.

"Zo'thre," she responded into his ear just as quietly.

Quinton pulled back and looked her in the eyes for the first time. It was unsettling but not as uncomfortable as Zo would have thought. She felt a warm tingle above her right breast.

"My mark," Quinton explained, pulling back from her. This close, she realized it wasn't mist circling around him but smoke and ash. It seemed to be radiating off of him. Zo kept eye contact with him, not backing down or wanting to be the first to look away. After a few moments of staring at each other, he pulled away, breaking their gaze.

"I'll be in touch then. To make good on our deal. See you soon, Zo'thre." He walked away from her and vanished into his smoke in a blink of an eye. If she hadn't known he'd been there a second ago, she would have never believed anyone else had ever been in this clearing.

Her name sounded odd on his lips but not unpleasant. Zo wondered how all this would turn out. But for now, she had to make her way back to Ze and see if Quinton did hold up his part of the bargain.

4

Chapter 4

Walking through the forest was easier this time. It was as if a weight had been lifted off her. Zo kept telling herself that Quinton would keep his promise. It was what Fae did. With that in mind, she couldn't help but let herself not be entirely at ease till she saw her brother again happy and healthy.

On her way there Zo felt alone in the forest. It wasn't that she was alone. The Nole Forest was full of animals and other people going about their lives. But she didn't feel like any of those things or people were there with her, now it felt as if she had someone there with her. It reminded her of when Ze and her were alone. Before that had found the others. It was the best way to describe it but it felt different. Not bad, but just different. She wondered if it was Quinton, he did say he was going to be keeping an eye on her.

She didn't sleep on the way back which meant she got back to the house much quicker than her trip out to the fae door. When their house was finally in view, she was running on pure adrenaline.

Zo had been too worried to sleep or eat much while she was

gone, and for the last two weeks, she'd hardly done so anyways. She was sure once Ze was up and well again she was going to sleep for days. But she couldn't think of that yet. For now, she just had to get home.

Bursting through the door, she made her way up to Ze's room. Her entrance to his bedroom must have sounded like a bomb went off at the force she pushed the door open causing it to slam into the wall.

She was greeted by a yelp from Primalis and a wahhh from Ze.

From the looks of it, Ze had been forced to stay in bed by Primalis as she continually brought him food. Zo had a feeling if it had been anyone else Ze would have just disregarded any and all words of warning saying he was fine.

And by the looks of it, Quinton had held up his end of the bargain. Ze looked amazing. If she hadn't been by his bedside for the last two weeks, Zo wouldn't have believed he had ever been sick. By the growing stack of bowls and plates that were starting to accumulate next to his bed, his apatite was back too. Primalis had happily given him as much food as he wanted. While Ze made up for lost time and meals.

"Thank the spirits you're alright," Zo said running over to her brother. She pulled him into a giant bear hug. Ze returned the hug knowing how worried she must have been about him.

"One moment, he was in the bed sweating with a high fever. The next, right as rain. It was magic. I still can't believe it," Primalis told her. She eyed Zo for a little longer than Zo was comfortable with. She had a feeling they would have a long talk later.

"Now if you ladies don't mind I have been in the same bed for two weeks and desperately need a bath," Ze told them ushering the women out of his room.

After being pushed out of the room, Primalis grabbed Zo's wrist and dragged her downstairs. When they were well enough away that Ze wouldn't hear them, she spun around to face Zo.

"You went to the fae door didn't you?" She was more accusing than asking. Her voice was a combination of fear and anger. Primalis had grown up in the wilds only leaving when her father felt it wasn't safe for her there anymore. Fae doors were standard in the wilds, and she was often told stories about what could happen if you dealt with the fae. But she was also taught, more importantly, how to avoid them.

"We were running out of options," Zo told her. She didn't have the same fear put into her as a child about the Fae, but Zo did know not to back out of a deal with them.

"Sallen and Wina are bringing back a blessed stone and holy water. And Gorran and Tesser are going after the lorec beast. The heart is supposed to cure anything. You just needed to wait. Either of those things could have hel-"

"But those things take time. Time Ze did not have!"

Gorran and Tesser were the other two members of their small make-it-your-self family. Gorran was a half-orc who wasn't the brightest but was definitely the most loving. He was the one who typically made sure everyone was fed and had clean clothes. Tesser was a lizardfolk who was a wizard. He much preferred libraries and laboratories to people and being outside. And because of that was usually the one who found jobs for them. Acting almost as their agent. He'd been frantically researching what could help Ze and found a creature whose heart was said to cure anything. So they'd gone after it.

Primalis let out a small sigh. Zo could tell she was torn between having Ze back to his healthy self and fearing what Zo had to trade for it.

"I know, but a deal?"

"It's fine. I made a deal. And it was on my terms."

"What was it for?"

For the second time today, Ze's door was slammed open. This time it was him who yelped. Primalis burst into the room, pulling Zo through the door after her. Ze was freshly back from the bath and thankfully had pants on.

"Tell him!" Primalis yelled at Zo, pulling her in front of her brother.

"Primalis, what's going on?" Ze asked. He was about to pull on his shirt but now just held it in front of him, almost as protection from Primalis and his sister.

"This really isn't a big deal. It was my decision. I'm an adult. I can-" Zo said trying to stay calm and rational about the situation.

"It has to do with him he has a right to know."

"As I said, he didn't have anything to do with it. He didn't have a say-"

"Zo'thre, please!" Primalis screamed at her, then more gently, "Tell your brother. He should know what's going to happen."

Ze looked expectantly at his sister not quite sure what he was supposed to do. Or whose side to take? After a brief sigh, Zo spoke.

"I made a deal with a fae. That's why you got better."

"Excuse me?!" Ze demanded. He dropped his shirt, now forgotten, and stepped towards her.

"You were sick for two weeks. Nothing was helping," Zo desperately tried to explain.

"So you what sold your soul?"

"I didn't sell my soul. I promised him a baby."

"That's worse! He's going to take away your child? And what will the father of this child say?"

"The father is taking it away."

"What!" Both Ze and Primalis screamed. Ze grabbed his sister's wrists and pulled them towards him.

"Tell me you didn't make a deal with a fae to have his baby, then give that baby to him," He desperately said.

"Then I won't."

There was silence in the room for a bit. Primalis' hands had gone to her mouth. She had only heard the part about Zo giving up her firstborn, not that her firstborn would be half-fae. Ze could only look at his sister. There were a few times they didn't automatically trust each other. It usually was when one of them did something without the other. They'd done things together for so long that doing something independently felt like a betrayal.

"It's just sex. I have sex all the time," Zo tried to reassure her brother. She pulled herself out of his grasp and rested her hand on his shoulder.

"But, this time, you need to get pregnant. And then you need to actually have the baby," Ze told her. He was trying to convince her this was a bad idea.

"I know."

"Are you willing to give up your child like that?"

"They'll be with their father. Our life isn't really conducive to children. It's dangerous."

Quiet went over the room again. Ze broke away from his sister and sat down on his bed. Primalis hadn't moved since she found out Zo would have a baby with a fae. She looked between the siblings, not sure what to do.

"What happens if you don't fill your end of the bargain?" Ze finally asked, eyes not leaving Zo.

"You go back to being sick. And at the rate you were going, you die," Zo told him. She never wanted bad news sugar-coated. None of her friends had said it, but everyone was thinking it. Ze had been dying.

"I made a choice, and I'm the one who has to live with the consequences no matter what they are," Zo told them when neither spoke. She turned to leave the room.

"I'm exhausted. I'm going to sleep. I'm glad you're better, Ze. I was worried."

As Zo left the room, Ze and Primalis exchanged glances. Ze pinched the bridge of his nose and let out an annoyed sigh.

"I should have never told her there was a fae door nearby. This is all my fault," Primalis said. It was obvious that she was taking all the blame on herself. It was a bad habit she had, and the rest of the group members did their best to reassure her when it happened.

"You didn't tell her to make the deal did you?" Ze questioned. His voice was quiet but loud enough for her to hear.

"Of course not. I'd never do that."

"Then how could it have been your fault?"

"I don't..."

"I'm going to find a way to get her out of the deal."

"I really don't think that's a good idea. We don't know what will happen."

Ze seemed to be thinking about different outcomes or different things he could do to fix his sister's problem

"Tesser would know."

"Maybe, but he's off trying to find something to help you," Ze explained "I'll send word to the others that you're better. It might take him a few days to get back."

Ze just nodded, but his mind was set he was going to get Zo out of her deal with the fae because nothing good ever came out of dealing with fairies.

5

Chapter 5

After all of the events of the last two weeks and everything in the last few hours, Zo was exhausted. She desperately needed a full night's sleep. She need more than a night she needed an entire week of just sleep and relaxation.

The best she was probably going to get was a night. Once everyone was back, they would need to work. For the last two weeks, everyone had been focused on taking care of Ze. Any jobs they could have worked were an afterthought, and the little money they'd put away was almost gone. Being an adventure definitely had its perks, but the uncertainty of finances sometimes definitely wasn't one of them.

Finally, alone Zo looked at herself in the mirror. She definitely looked tired and like she'd traveled nonstop for the last few days, but besides that, she didn't look any different. If she didn't know any better no one would know she'd made a deal with a fae. That was when she remembered the mark.

She touched above her right breast. Nothing felt different. The tingling that had been there was long gone now. So she undid her front laces and removed her jacket and leathers. Coming down to her shirt. She unlaced the top and pulled the oversized collar to the side. And just as Quinton had promised there was a mark there. It meant she was protected by him till their deal was done.

If you didn't know any better the make looked like a very interesting birthmark or a fading tattoo. It was a wiry tree with lots of branches reaching in all directions. And in the center of the trunk was a cut out of a four-pointed star.

She touched it lightly. There was no raise to the skin like there would be if it was a tattoo. It felt like just another part of her skin. She guessed it was part of her now.

Kicking off her boots and pulling off her shirt. Zo was just down to her stays and camise. She undid her stays and threw all her clothes randomly around her room. After a long rest, she'd deal with them, but for now, she needed sleep.

As she drifted off, the sound of the wind running through branches lulled her into a restful sleep. She thought it slightly odd since her window was closed but was too tired to question it much.

The sleep was much needed, and the only reason she woke up in the middle of the night was her stomach demanded food.

Making her way to the kitchen the rest of the house was asleep. She heard her brother snoring behind his closed door. It was a welcome sound over the gasping and heavy breathing that had been the only noise coming out of his room for the last two weeks.

She didn't feel like making anything too labor-intensive currently. So settled on bread with some meat and cheese. It wasn't anything extraordinary or great but it hit the spot. The last thing of any substance that she had eaten was the stew Primalis had made a few days ago. On the road, she'd eaten dried meats and nuts mostly. The fresh bread and meat were a nice change of pace.

After appeasing her stomach, she made her way back to her room going to get some more much-needed sleep. She guessed she'd been sleeping for about seven or eight hours at this point, but that would only put a small dent into her broken sleep pattern over the last two weeks.

Opening the door, Zo realized she was no longer alone in her room. Sitting on the bed was a figure. Her first instinct was to fight, but she only had on her camise and the closest weapon was leaning against the wall a few feet away.

"I was hoping to find you sleeping," Quinton said turning towards the door as it opened.

"I fell asleep before dinner and was hungry," Zo told him. She dropped her stance and made her way into the room, closing the door behind her.

"Feeling better now?" He rose from the bed, walking toward her. The question surprised her. She didn't think her well-being would be high on his list.

"Does it really matter?"

"You are to be the mother of my child so you being in good health is import and if we are to have sex you should be rested and have energy."

"You're very pragmatic about this whole thing."

"That may be but I do fully intend to hold up my end of the bargain. And the sooner we are to start the less stressful it will be."

He'd made his way over to her, now inches away. She could feel his body heat this close. She wouldn't say hot, but it was a few degrees warmer than her. He was almost a good half a foot taller than her. She would have to look up at him just for everyday conversation. The smoke that had been ever-present around him in the forest didn't seem to be there at all now. It could just be the low light, but there was no swirl around him like earlier.

"You make a very valid point. You sure you're alright sleeping with a half-elf?" Zo asked trying not to let on how curious she was about sleeping with a fae. She was by no means a virgin. And had been, as some would say, adventurous in her choices of partners. But that was more who was offering at the time when she was in need or want.

"As long as you're fine sleeping with a Fae," He responded. She didn't say anything and just went on her tiptoes, bringing her mouth closer to him. Still too short to reach him fully, Quinton met her halfway. Once their lips touched, it was like someone had given them all systems go signal.

They no longer coyly danced around the idea that they were about to have sex. Quinton's fingers went into Zo's hair. She'd pulled it out of her tight bun to sleep, but it was still loosely plated together. It was loose enough that he could grip it and gain some control over her. He knew there would be no fully controlling Zo, but that was something he liked about her. She wouldn't be fully controlled by anyone.

Her hands had gone to his chest pulling at his shirt. He wore a loose jacket over it and she needed it off. She wanted all of his clothes off, but she would start with his jacket. When she felt him start to grip her hair, she knew he was definitely wearing too much clothing.

"Clothes off," Zo managed to say, pulling away from him. Instead of taking off his clothes, he started to kiss her neck. It was gentle and soft; after a few kisses and licks, it became rough and needy. He pushed her against her now-closed door while putting his knee in between her legs.

The hand not in her hair began to roam over her body, finding its way to the bottom of her camise. It then began working its way under and up. She couldn't help but start to grind against his leg. Even with Zo's colorful sexual past, it had been a while. And it had definitely been a very long time since someone was so attentive.

"Quinton," She managed to say between moans and gasps. He visibly stiffened at the sound of his name. He stopped and came up from her neck looking her in the eyes. Even in the low light, she could see his unnatural blues.

"My name, it. It holds power..." He told her drifting off. Zo understood. For Fae, their name had power over them. Anyone who had their name had power over them. But the same was true for any name they knew. She had power over him. But in turn, he had power over her. It must be uncomfortable for him for her to say it so casually.

"Sorry... Quin," She said almost in a whisper. He was close enough to hear, though.

"That works," He said before kissing her lips again. As enjoyable as being kissed and man-handled against her door was. And yes, Zo was very much enjoying herself. She wanted more. She needed more.

She managed to wiggle out of his grasp, grabbed his wrist, and started pulling him towards her bed.

"A little impatient?" His voice had a joking tone, but she could tell it was a legitimate question. As if she was asking if she was sure she wanted to do this. Even though she had already told him yes, he still ensured she was positive. Almost as if he was willing to call off the whole deal if she said she didn't want this.

"Aren't you? If that kiss was any indicator. I'm surprised

either of us still has any clothes on."

"I promise to take everything off soon, but first, lay back."

Zo was now sitting on her bed and looking up at him. She was hoping he was talking about what she thought he was talking about. Quinton knelt at the side of her bed, grabbed her hips, and dragged her toward him. Positioning her in front of him. He then pushed up her camise to her stomach.

Quinton started kissing, licking, and biting his way up her thigh, wanting to enjoy this as much as he hoped Zo would. He was rewarded with sounds of enjoyment from her. Which only made him want to tease her more.

Once he reached her pelvis, he pulled back slightly so he was only just brushing her entrance and folds. Making sure to lightly blow on them. Causing her to let out a noise between enjoyment and annoyance. It then became more pleasure as his right hand gripped the top of her thigh so his thumb could lightly brush her sensitive bud. He then made his way down the other leg. Repeating the process of kissing, licking, and biting, only this time down her leg.

Going down to her knee, he then came back up to her entrance. His tongue replaced his thumb on her bud. His reward was a sharp intake of air, and one of Zo's hands slid into his hair.

Not wanting to disappoint, his left hand slid under her camise and up to her breast. It was a good weight in his hand. He hadn't expected her to have this large of a cup size since her leather armor and stays had done more to hide them than he expected. In no way was she complaining. It was just a surprise.

Quinton found her nipple and started to roll it between his fingers. She let out a moan, and her breathing became more labored. It sounded like she was trying to say something he couldn't quite make out. But the way her figures gripped his hair and pushed him closer toward her told him everything he needed to know.

Sucking on her bud a little more before moving toward her folds. His tongue worked its way around her folds much to Zo's displeasure. As much as she liked him teasing her, this was getting out of hand. She was more sensitive than she had been in a long while, and at this point, she desperately needed him. Without him even touching her, she was already sopping wet. A fact that was not lost on Quinton and made him want to tease her more, but there was always later or another time.

He made a mental note that he was thinking about another time already. He was here to get her pregnant, not to get attached. He pushed those thoughts out of his mind saying it had been a while since he'd thoroughly enjoyed something, and this was something he was fully enjoying.

Well, in this case, someone. But for now, he decided not to think about it and just continue to enjoy it and make Zo enjoy it.

Pinching her nipple harder, he slid a finger into her as his tongue licked her. He could feel how wet she had become just by his teasing. It made him want to keep doing things to her. It was like he'd been given a new toy that did all sorts of things he didn't know about. Every new thing made him even more excited, and he couldn't wait to find out more.

The grip on Quinton's hair got tighter, and Zo's other hand that had been gripping the bed sheets darted to the back of his neck. Pulling him closer to her. Not wanting to disappoint, he happily obliged. Along with adding another finger, he licked her from bottom to top. Making sure to give extra attention to her bud. Which was under a consent attack by his thumb. Quinton felt her cum more than anything, but that's not saying Zo was quiet.

A loud scream of pleasure echoed through the room. When the sound faded and her grip slacked, he couldn't help but smile. There was a bit of pride there, making him feel like he did a good job. His next plan of attack was to lick and bite everything in sight, but before he could. Quinton felt Zo pulling him up to her.

"I need you inside me," She told him after a quick kiss. He couldn't help but smile. It was very nice to be needed.

Pulling back, Quinton quickly pulled his shirt off and then made quick work of his pants. Looking down at Zo, she had pulled off her camise and was now fully naked. The moonlight highlighted her curves and made her look almost otherworldly. She was flush from the orgasm he'd just given her. And her eyes were filled with need and desire for him. He couldn't help but stare at her. She reached up her arms to him, beckoning him back to her.

Falling back into her arms, he kissed her. It was hard and heavily full of need and want. If someone had told Quinton he was going to be in this position before he had met Zo, he wouldn't have believed them. But now he couldn't think of anywhere else he wanted to be. He was finding comfort in this half-elf.

Pulling away slightly, he aligned himself with her. Thrusting into her. Zo let out something between a gasp and a moan. He slid in with no resistance she had been completely ready for him.

It was not long before they were both breathing hard and close to release. Zo wraped her arms around him, clinging and pulling him closer. Quinton picked up the already fast pace being even more forceful if that was even possible. This caused a deep moan to spill from her lips as she threw her head back.

All the noises she was making only spurred him on. Wanting to hear more. But that would have to wait for another time. He was close.

Letting out a yell, Quinton began to shake as he spilled his seed into Zo. It's a combination of disappointment and relief. He wanted to keep going, but it felt so good to fill her like this.

Losing all energy, he fell on top of her. It wasn't a bad weight, Zo realized, enjoying it. His breathing was still uneven as he started to catch it.

She can't help but pull her arms around him. Pulling himself out of her, Quinton relaxed into the embrace. Neither wanting to move or really having the energy to, they drifted asleep wrapped in each other's arms.

6

Chapter 6

The morning sun cut across the bed, waking Zo up. She had purposely picked this room and put her bed in this spot so the sun would wake her up at the same time every day. It wasn't too early but left her with plenty of morning before she had to start her day. Turning over was when she remembered she wasn't alone in her bed.

Quinton was still asleep, and it was the first time she'd seen him relax. It was as if he was constantly wearing a mask or keeping people deliberately away. But here he looked somewhat peaceful.

Zo didn't want to wake him up but knew she couldn't stay here all day. She reached over to gently brush her fingers against his cheek. Before she could touch him Quinton's eyes shot open and he pulled back from her quickly. It took him a second to realize where he was but instantly relaxed when his brain caught up with his body.

"Sorry about that," he said, letting out a breath that Zo could only guess was to try and calm himself down.

"It's fine. I'm not used to sleeping next to someone else

either," She told him, not taking any offense to his reaction. Quinton couldn't help but let his eyes drift to his mark above her right breast. It looked good on her, and a little voice inside of him told him that it meant she was his. He tried to bat away the voice. Telling it she just had a deal with him. And he was here filling his role in that deal. Nothing more, nothing less.

"Yeah, it's been a while." His voice was low and if Zo hadn't been listening, she would have missed it. Silence hung between them for a few seconds neither of them knowing quite what to do.

Then Quinton sat up fully and pulled himself out of bed as gracefully as possible. Zo made a face of annoyance. It wasn't directed at him it was more that she would have to get up too. And she wasn't sure if she was ready to face everyone yet. It was easy to forget that she would have to deal with the rest of her friends when they all returned. Also, it was highly likely that her conversation with both Ze and Primalis was not over.

The idea of having to go through the "it's life, my choice, and what's done is done" speech again was definitely not something she was looking forward to.

Getting up from the bed, Zo started getting dressed. She'd put all her clothes in the same place she normally did in her room, on top of her chest. But her camis had been discarded somewhere without much thought last night it took a few extra seconds to find.

Not knowing how he'd done it, Quinton was dressed and fully put together. Zo on the other hand just had her camise and pants on neither will were tied and her hair was a fluff of bedhead. She chucked up his put-togetherness to his faeness which was the only explanation she could come up with.

"How long till you know if you're pregnant?" Quinton asked

her, making sure his coat looked nice.

"I'll know in about three weeks, but you know it normally doesn't happen the first time," Zo told him, starting to lace up her pants.

"You're saying we'll need to do this again?"

"Is that a problem?"

"No, no. More of an observation."

"Then I'll be seeing you again soon, or did you want to wait and see if I get my monthly blood."

"Well, if having more sex means a higher chance of pregnancy then I think that is the best course of action."

"Then I'll see you soon."

Quinton only nodded and then was gone. He was there one moment then just gone the next. If he hadn't been standing in front of Zo, she wouldn't have believed he was there. Instead, thinking their midnight sexcapades had been more of a dream than anything real. The slight ache she now had told her it had been anything but a dream and all too real. It wasn't a bad ache, just a gentle reminder of their night.

First things first, she needed a bath. Then breakfast. After that, she'd deal with whatever her brother or friends wanted to say to her. For now, she just wanted to get somewhat back to the land of the living.

After a quick bath and getting fully dressed Zo finally made her way downstairs. It was still relatively early but not the crack of dawn that Primalis and Tesser got up at. How either of them could rise that early was still unknown to her.

She could hear voices on the other side of the kitchen door. She didn't think anyone else was back yet, so it had to be Primalis and Ze. When she opened the door, they instantly stopped talking. Which didn't overly sit well with her. She know neither of them was happy about the deal and figured they would be extra annoyed if they know Quinton had been there last night.

Deciding the best course of action or the course Zo most wanted to take was flat-out ignoring the whole thing. She went to the cupboard to make herself breakfast, some oats and berries sounded good.

She could feel eyes on her, but if it was one or both of them, she wasn't sure. It wasn't till she started preparing her breakfast that the silence was finally broken.

"You're really just going to pretend nothing is happening?" Ze asked angrily.

"What else am I supposed to do?" She responded, turning towards him.

"I don't know fight against it."

"If I do that you die."

Ze tried to say something only to be cut off by Zo.

"I made a deal. I made a choice I have to live with it. And I don't regret that choice. Now respect that decision or don't it's your choice but I don't want to hear about it. It was my life Ze'zein. You would have done it for me."

Ze looked like he wanted to say something but kept it to himself. Primalis was never one to want any confrontation, and she tried to change the subject.

"I got a message that there is a small bugbear problem on the west side of town. We three could take care of it before the others come back."

"It'd be good to do some work and get out of the house," Zo told her trying to sound cheery and not like she was fighting with her twin.

"Getting out of the house would be nice," Ze agreed.

The three of them walked to the west side of town. It was no surprise they had a monster problem. The west side of town was used as a storage and dumping area. It would often attract smaller monsters. For the most part, the people that worked here could take care of them but bugbears weren't considered small and could inflict some damage if push came to shove. It was best to leave it up to adventures or mercenaries.

It looked like it would be a simple job which, honestly they could use. Primalis and Zo were still sleep-deprived, and one night of decent sleep would not fix that. Ze, even though he was completely cured, was still weary of not overdoing it, especially since he didn't trust the fae magic.

"There's only two. This should be easy. Ze and I will go in from opposite sides, Primalis see if you can hold them down with some vines," Zo told them. There was an unwritten rule that she was in charge during combat. Mainly because she made the best plans out of everyone. But was always open to ideas and input from others.

Ze and Zo darted off to the side of the bugbears while Primalis called vines to grapple the bears down. Luckily they had been distracted by rummaging through the dumping piles, so Primalis was able to restrain them with no trouble.

On the left, Zo hit the one closest to her with three consecutive arrows right in the throat. From the right, Ze through his daggers at the other one. Both the bugbears were injured, but they weren't down yet. The bears pulled against Primalis' vines, trying to get free, but she held them steady. The strain was getting to her, though. They were strong, and it took a lot of energy to keep them there. The twins were going to need to move fast if they wanted to do this without having a full-blown fistfight with a bear.

Ze ran towards his bugbear and grabbed the daggers that were lodged in its side. He then pulled them down and across, gutting the animal.

Zo also ran towards the creature she'd shot her arrows at. She hurried up its back and shot an arrow into its skull and the in both its eyes.

The two animals let out roars of pain before going silent. They both lay still, breathing their last breath. It hadn't been a hard fight, but it could have easily gone wrong if they weren't a well-oiled machine used to working together. After a lifetime of working with her brother and years working with Primalis, this was something Zo never had to worry about. They always got the job done, even if it wasn't always this clean.

Now that the bugbears were taken care of, they just needed to show proof of the kill and report it to a clean-up team. That was the easy part. It wasn't a lot of money, but it was some money, and since they hadn't worked at all in the last two weeks, they definitely needed all the jobs they could get.

As Zo walked away from them toward the fallen monsters, she felt like someone was watching her. It wasn't unsettling, and it was slightly familiar. She wondered if Quinton was keeping tabs on her to ensure she could uphold her end of their deal. She couldn't fill it if she was dead.

7

Chapter 7

The rest of the day was uneventful. Primalis and Ze had taken to avoiding talking about Zo's fae deal. Zo could tell they still didn't like it but knew if they tried to talk to her about it there wouldn't be any progress. So they didn't. The conversation that did happen was mostly Primalis trying to fill the space.

The constant talking about nothing really was wearing to Zo, but Ze didn't seem to mind at all as words kept coming out of her mouth. Zo remembered how she'd taken care of Ze when he was sick. Primalis had also slept next to him any nights that Zo hadn't. It was odd watching two people fall in love.

Ze and Zo had always only had each other. Over the last few years, they'd found friends to also rely on, and both had found others to warm their beds. But when it all boiled down, they only really relied on each other. It felt like he was leaving her.

She felt a slight pull at her heart every time she looked at them. She wasn't sure if it was concern, jealousy, or sadness. Most definitely she did not want to admit it might be happiness that her twin had found someone in this complex world. Especially not someone who'd seen all of him over the last few years and was there. Someone who'd seen all his good and bad and said I still want that.

The next few days passed without much incident. The three of them did a few jobs around town while waiting for the others to return. They'd send messages to them saying the Ze had made a full recovery. The information of how he got better was left to be told. Zo had made it clear she did not want to talk about it anymore, and she wasn't going to try and change her mind.

Sallen and Wina were the first ones back. Zo had been in town when they returned, and either Ze or Primalis must have told them what was going on because when she got home, they both gave her a look of almost pity.

Zo could handle a lot of nasty looks but pity was one she really didn't want to deal with.

"They told you," was all she said, putting down the basket of food she'd gotten in town. She didn't mind that they knew it was more she didn't want to have the same conversation over and over again. One time was enough.

"Told us what?" Sallen asked. By the tone in his voice, she could tell he knew about her deal.

"That I made a deal with a fae."

"No! You didn't." Sallen's voice was strained, and Zo knew he was pretending to be surprised by this news.

"Stop it, Sallen. Yes, they told us. I can't say I agree, but I understand. If you need any help with anything, let me know. I mean, as things progress with said pregnancy," Wina told her. Wina was typically the one who understood everyone's choices were their own. Even though she was religious and held deep beliefs beyond her religious ones, she never forced them on any members of her party.

It was nice to know she would be there to help Zo as much as she needed it. Zo hoped the others would come around by the time she was pregnant, but she knew she wasn't guaranteed anything. And she didn't want to force anything on them.

"Well, I know pregnancy can be weird. I'm the oldest of 15 siblings. So I have a bunch of home remedies my mom used when she was pregnant. My sisters all have used them too. So what I'm saying is I'm here for you too," Sallen told her. He wasn't the best when it came to talking about personal stuff or being sweet. Sarcasm and jokes were his defense, but in the rare moments he was sweet it was nice, and you knew it was genuine.

"I appreciate that, both of you. It means a lot to know I have support," Zo told them. It was very nice not to have to defend herself again. She wasn't looking forward to talking to Tesser, who would have all sorts of options on the matter. Gorran, on the other hand, would probably default to trusting her judgment as usual. But he got oddly protective of everyone in the group and hoped this wouldn't be one of those times. Especially since Ze already wanted to kill Quinton.

After catching up a bit with Sallen and Wina, Zo finally made it back to her room. It had been a long day of working and running errands. She just wanted to relax before dinner.

It didn't surprise her that Quinton was waiting on her bed when she got back to her room, but it did make her wonder what type of schedule he kept. She knew he'd been watching her whenever she went out, and it felt like she wasn't alone when she fell asleep at night. After their first night together, he hadn't come back to visit since.

He looked up at her with an almost happy expression. She could never really tell what he was thinking because almost no emotion showed on his face. She didn't know if it was just a fae thing or more of a Quinton thing. He seemed to hold back all his emotions, and only a few slipped through when he wasn't paying attention. Almost as if he'd been told his whole life that this was how you had to present yourself.

"It's been a few days. I was wondering when you were going to be back," Zo said, pulling off her jacket and getting more comfortable.

"I had a few things to take care of. People always get nosy when a fae door appears. I moved after our conversation," he told her, not getting up from her bed. Instead, he leaned back and watched her as if to get more comfortable while he watched a show.

"I take it you're here to continue our deal then?"

"And if I am?"

"It's easier if you come at night."

"It is night."

"I mean later in the night. Everyone is expecting me for dinner."

"I quite enjoyed our last... interaction. Even if it's shorter than last time, I can also come back later."

"You know both can be an option."

Zo was down to just her pants and camise now. She walked over to him and crawled onto the bed, her legs straddling him.

"I do like the sound of that."

Quinton's hands instantly went to her waist. His left one gripped her, pulling her closer, and the right one started to move up her back. Zo draped her arms over his shoulders, allowing him to bring her closer.

Their lips lightly grazed each others. It was as if neither wanted to admit how much they wanted this. If Zo was being honest, she'd thought about him every day since the night he'd come to her room. Every night wondering if this would be the one he came to her again. Quinton couldn't get the half-elf out of his mind either. No matter how hard he had tried. Staying away only seemed to make it worse, and he couldn't take it anymore. He needed her, wanted her, and she was his to take.

He forcefully pulled her closer. Happy to find her so willing to deepen their kiss. He fell back onto the bed, bringing her with him.

She started to unlace his shirt as he pulled her's off her. There was a little delay at the point of both of them struggling out of their pants. It wasn't graceful in any sense of the word, but neither of them cared. They only cared that they were not currently naked.

Now both fully naked and ready, Zo jumped on top of him. When he sat up to try and position her under him, she pulled him back down on the bed. He'd been on top last time. It was her turn. She wanted to give him a bit of show.

Already wet and wanting, she positioned herself above him. He was hard and just as wanting as she was. With one quick motion, she slid him into her. Filling her as no one else had before.

Zo looked down at Quinton, letting out a moan of pure pleasure and enjoyment. If he had enjoyed himself last time, this time was on a completely different level. He loved everything about this.

"You alright with this?" Zo asked almost jokingly. The look on his face told her everything. He'd probably start arguing if she tried to change positions.

"Don't you dare change anything," was all Quinton said as he thrust his hips up to meet hers.

The force and movement earned him a moan of pleasure.

Catching her breath, Zo rested her hands on his chest and started to move her hips.

Quinton couldn't do anything but try and catch his breath and watch her. He rested his hands on her hips, gripping her skin hard enough to leave marks. He could feel her move against him, slowly starting to pick up the pace.

Zo's hair had fallen out of her loose braid, and it cascaded down around her shoulders. As much as Quinton liked the slightly disheveled look she had currently, it was getting in the way of seeing her lovely breasts. He reached up and moved one side of her hair behind her shoulder. So he could fully see her. After lightly caressing her cheek, he moved his hand down to cup her breast.

Slightly pinching her nipple just made Zo go faster. Understanding now that her hair had been in the way, she moved the rest out of the way. Quinton couldn't help but smile at this. Not only could he fully see her chest, but he could also proudly see his mark on display. He liked seeing it on her.

When he first put it on her, it was truly just so he could find her without any trouble. But now, it was starting to mean more. At least it meant more to him.

He started to feel himself reaching his climax but didn't want to get there before Zo did. So he pinched her nipple more and slid his other hand toward her bud. Stroking small circles on it to bring her closer to climax. His efforts paid off.

Zo's whole body shook as she let out a long, almost painful moan. She fell forward, propping herself up on her elbows on either side of his head.

"Everything alright?" Quinton asked in almost a joking manner.

"Great," She managed to breathe out. She hardly had any

breath left in her.

"Hold on then."

He then wrapped his arms around her pulling her closer. Thrusting up into her. It only took a few till he, too, came. He'd been close already, and seeing her like that made it even easier for him.

Both their breathing was ragged and uneven. They stayed in each other's arms longer than either of them thought the other would let them. It was nice. More comfortable than either of them wanted to admit.

A knock at the door broke the comfortable spell that had set around them.

"Zo, dinner's ready. You coming down?" Ze said from the other side of the door.

"Yeah, I'll be right down. I'm just changing," She yelled at the door.

"'Kay." they could hear Ze's footsteps walking away from the door and down the hall.

Zo let out a sigh and pulled herself away from Quinton. As hungry as she was, the desire to stay in the bed with him was great. She let out another sigh as she started to pick up her clothes.

Quinton walked up behind her and rested his hands on her waist. It startled her, but at the same time felt nice to be back so close to him.

"I have a few things to take care of. I'll be back later tonight," He whispered in her ear as his breath tickled her neck.

"Alright, I'll see you in a bit," Zo told him. She turned to catch his lips. It wasn't a deep kiss or one of their more passionate ones like they shared during sex but still a nice kiss. It made them both stop for a moment.

"I'll see you soon," Quinton said, pulling away. His hand lingered on her cheek before pulling that away too. Then he was gone. Zo couldn't help but smile.

She quickly pulled on her clothes and then made her look somewhat presentable. And she was out the door and down to the kitchen for dinner.

8

Chapter 8

Not knowing when Quinton was going to be back, Zo slid into her bed without waiting for him. She could still smell him on her sheets from his earlier visit. It was a nice reminder and brought a smile to Zo's lips. It was getting harder and harder to push her thoughts of him aside.

After only seeing him three times, two of which they slept together, she couldn't get him out of her head. It was as if he'd purposely made her have thoughts about him. Even though she knew Fae had powers, she didn't know to what extent. Could they make people fall in love with them or at least always want to be around them?

Or was it this mark that was on her chest?

Whatever it was, she would have to figure it out or ask Quinton. But asking him might cause problems. No, she just needed to get pregnant and then give him a baby. He would leave, and they both could go on with their lives.

Hopefully, Ze would also come around and actually talk to her. He seemed to be making more conversation with Primals than her currently. She didn't know if it was because he actually wanted to talk to her over his own sister. Or if this was a product of the deal she made on his behalf. They used to do everything together and be near inseparable, but everything was changing now. Zo didn't know if it was for the better or not.

She didn't even feel Quinton slide into bed next to her until his arms wrapped around her. She had been so lost in her thoughts that she didn't notice him arrive.

When he'd seen her tucked nicely into bed, he couldn't help but join her. It had been a long day of dealing with people who either just wanted to bother him or weren't willing to make a decent deal. One group of people came wanting to kill him, stating that all fae were evil.

Now he knew fae had a reputation but not everyone was bad. He kept his deals fair and only asked for children if he knew he could take care of them. The last one was over 50 years ago, and they were completely grown up now. Off having their own adventures.

Snuggling next to her was nice. He still wasn't sure why this half-elf had grown on him so much. But he was beginning not to care. If he was able to have this waiting for him after a long day, everything probably would be easier.

His arms going around her startled Zo a little, but then she relaxed into them. He felt nice. It did surprise her that he wasn't trying to instantly have sex with her. But decided not to bring it up. It had been a while since she'd slept in anyone's arms. And even longer since it had been a lover.

Quinton was the first to wake up this time. He had to remind himself he was in Zo's room. Still not used to sleeping anywhere but his own bed. It was still very odd to him to wake up next to her. Not a bad odd just different.

Zo was quietly sleeping next to him. He knew she'd been working almost nonstop since her brother had improved over the last few days. She must have been tired. He had completely planned on having sex with her again when he came back last night but she'd looked so comfortable and inviting he couldn't help himself.

This morning as well, sex was the furthest thing from his mind. He was just enjoying the early morning cuddles.

It was a nice feeling to wake up with Quinton's arms around her. Zo liked having him in bed with her. It was oddly comfortable and relaxing. She didn't want to get too attached since he'd just leave her once she had the baby. But for now, at least she could enjoy the feeling.

"How'd you sleep?" He asked, feeling her start to wake up.

"Like a rock. I hardly remember you coming in last night," Zo told him, rolling over so she could face him.

"It looked like you needed it. You've been working almost nonstop."

"Well, that's what happens when you don't work for two weeks. I have to make up for lost time."

"I guess I don't really know, though."

"I guess you wouldn't fae don't really follow the same rules as everyone else."

"We follow rules. They're just our own. And we don't live in this world."

"True."

Zo reached up her arms to stretch. She didn't miss Quintion checking her out as she did so.

"Enjoying the show," She asked half-jokingly.

"I am, actually."

Zo couldn't help but let out a laugh. Quinton took this

opportunity to lean over and kiss her. He then ran his hand down from her cheek all the way to the end of her camise down by her thigh.

"You know if you ever need help while working, you can call me," he told her after pulling away from their kiss.

"Protecting your investment?"

"No, it's not that...I just-"

"I'm joking," Zo said, cutting him off. "If you're not careful, I might think you're getting attached."

"And we wouldn't want that now, would we."

Zo just smiled and kissed him. Neither one of them really wanted to go down that line of questioning. Because neither one was ready to admit they were getting attached.

Quinton's hand started going up her leg under her camise. As his hands began to wander, so did hers. He'd pulled off all his clothes last night except some lose fitting pants.

At that moment, when they were pulling off each other's clothes, Zo's bedroom door swung open.

"Gorran and Tesser just got back, they said they...saw...a..." Ze said, walking into her room. His words started to fail him as he realized what he had just walked into.

"You're the fae that tricked my sister!" Ze yelled as soon as his eyes fell on Quinton. Zo just let out a sigh and brought her hand to her face in annoyance.

"I think she tricked me more than anything," Quinton told Ze.

"Ze, we've talked about this," She said, still annoyed.

"You're still going through with this. I didn't ask because I didn't want to know-" Ze kept saying as if they hadn't said anything.

"Get out!" Zo yelled, pushing off the blankets to get out of bed.

"-what you were doing. But, I thought at least you'd think about it before having a fae in your-" Ze kept going, not listening to his sister.

"Out," Zo said while pushing him out of her room and slamming the door behind him. She made sure it was locked this time. She could still hear her brother yelling through the door but tried to ignore him as she made her way back to the bed and Quinton.

9

Chapter 9

Zo flopped back onto the bed with an annoyed sigh.

"I take it your brother is not too pleased with our deal?" Quinton asked her.

"Not particularly. He feels like I betrayed him because I didn't talk to him first before doing it."

"You're twins, I have a feeling your lives haven't diverged much up to this point."

"Not really, no. But they're starting to."

"It happens."

"Yeah..."

They laid in bed for a little bit. Ze had given up yelling at the door, but they hadn't heard him walk away yet. Zo bet he was just sitting there waiting for her to come out. Part of her wanted to try and climb out the window.

"Well, I guess I better get up the last two members of our group got back. I'm sure they also have opinions of our deal," Zo told him, sitting up. She got out of bed and started to pull on her clothes.

"What do you think the chances are your brother will try and kill me if I walk out the front door?" Quinton asked as he started to get dressed as well. Like last time he was fully dressed and ready in an instant. As he waited for Zo to finish, he watched her getting dressed enjoying the time it took her and how her fingers worked.

"Low, but I have a feeling the yelling isn't over."

"I can take yelling."

Surprisingly Ze wasn't outside Zo's door when they opened it. She walked Quinton to the front door and said, goodbye. She could feel the others watching her from their "hiding places" But decided to ignore them till Quinton was gone.

After saying goodbye, he walked out the door and towards the woods. Even though he could instantly travel where he was going, sometimes he liked to walk for a bit.

"Why are you staying around my sister?"

Ze was propped against the side of the house. He had been banking on the fact that Zo would have insisted that the fae walked out the door since he'd walked in on them.

"I don't quite know what you mean," Quinton responded.

"I know you two are going to have sex. That's the deal. She has your baby. But why are you just spending time with her? It's obvious you slept over last night."

"Your sister is a grown woman. What she does in her personal time is her business and responsibility."

"Fae never do anything without getting something in return. So why are you doing more than just sleeping with her? What do you want?"

"Who said I'm not getting anything out of this arrangement? Also, to answer your other questions, all I'll say is your sister is a very beautiful woman. Have a good day Ze."

With that, Quinton walked away with a wave.

CHAPTER 9

Ze was annoyed. More annoyed than when he found them in bed together. Fae never gave straight answers, and Zo definitely wasn't going to talk to him about this. They knew each other slept with other people but never went into any detail about it. They had an unspoken understanding it was something neither of them really wanted to talk about.

Tesser was in his bedroom, which was more like a study or library that happened to have a bed in it. Ze wanted to talk to him about Zo's deal. If anyone knew what to do about it, it would be him. Knocking on the doorframe, Ze let him know he was there.

"Ze great did you talk tell Zo about the dungeon we found. A great find, right? Should give us a nice payday. And I bet you'll find wonderful specimens for me," Tesser said. He definitely was a talker. Which could be grading on a person, but the group was quite used to it by now. But, Ze needed to get him on the correct topic.

"Not yet. I needed to ask you first. What do you know about fae deals?" Ze asked crossing his arms and leaning against the door frame.

"Fea deals? Why are you asking about that? You aren't thinking about making one, are you? Very tricky things."

"No, I'm not thinking about making one. I was wondering if there was a way to get out of them."

"If you're not thinking about making one why do you want to know?"

"Call it curiosity."

"Ah! Knowledge for knowledge's sake. Well as far as I know and have studied the only way to get out of a fae deal is if the fae and the person they made the deal with both agree to end it."

"What would happen to the thing the person got out of that

deal?"

"Not sure. I guess whatever they decided. Fae are notorious tricksters and hard to work with. Their only powers are their deals and words, so they must use them well. The only other thing is their name."

"What do you mean by their name?"

"Well, if you find out their true name, then you can control them. I guess you could force them to end a deal that way. But, I don't know of anyone who didn't have repercussions for using a fae's real name."

"Thanks, I'll tell Zo about the dungeon. We'll see about going in the next day or two."

"Excellent! Do you want me to look into fae more? We could talk more about them. I do always like a discussion on new topics."

"Sure, I think that's a good idea."

After saying goodbye to Tesser, he made his way back to the kitchen, where he figured Zo would be. She usually didn't do well without breakfast, and he didn't want to deal with a cranky sister if he didn't have to. She was probably already annoyed at him coming into her room this morning.

Luckily she was already eating when he walked in. She raised an eyebrow at him when he came in, almost as if she dared him to say something else. Considering she didn't want to talk about it and had decided she was just going to have this fae's kid, he would have to work on it behind her back. He just needed to make sure she didn't find out what he was doing, or she'd be really mad at him.

"What did you want to tell me when you rudely came into my room this morning?" Zo finally asked after eating most of her breakfast.

"Tesser and Gorran found a dungeon on their way back. It looks like it hasn't been touched in a while. It'd probably be a good place to check out. Even if there's no treasure, there are probably monsters we could get stuff of to sell," told her, trying not to take offense to her annoyed tone.

"Sounds like it'd be a good bet. Should all of us go?"

"It'd be the best bet. Tesser's going to see if there's any standing orders or bounties that have to do with it."

"Even if there's not, it'll be a good place to check out. You never know what you'll find in a dungeon."

She got up to leave, now done with breakfast. When she walked past Ze to exit the kitchen, he stopped her.

"About this morning."

"Ze, please drop it. This is what's happening. We're not little kids anymore. You don't need to protect me from everything."

He let out a sigh knowing if he kept pushing, it would get harder and harder to get through to her. He let her go.

Primalis found him sitting at the kitchen table by himself. It looked like Ze hadn't moved in a while.

"Everything alright?" Primalis asked as she placed a hand on his shoulder. He let out a long sigh and put his hand on top of hers.

"I guess I just thought Zo would follow my lead if I wasn't happy with something," Ze told her. It was difficult to stop thinking like it was them against the world. A few years ago, all they needed was to say one word, and both of them would turn tail and change course. But now they both were walking in different directions and making their own lives. He wasn't sure if he was completely happy about it. But he couldn't deny that he liked Primalis's company. He wanted to keep being around her for as long as possible.

"I guess that's what happens as time goes on and people get older. Things change." She gave his shoulder a reassuring squeeze.

"I know, but it doesn't mean I have to like it."

Primalis couldn't help but give him a small but sad smile and wrap her arms around him. It was hard to watch someone you cared about go through internal turmoil and not be able to do anything about it.

10

Chapter 10

Later that afternoon, all of them were sitting around the table to plan their trip to the dungeon. They would need to gather supplies and figure out timetables to make sure they didn't get trapped down there unprepared.

For the trip, it would take about half a day to get to the dungeon then they weren't sure how big it was besides from a few assessments from Tesser, he thought it would take them about three or four days to get through it. Then about a day or two to get back out. So they would need about a week and a half's worth of supplies just to be on the safe side. It was always better to have too much stuff than not enough.

Each member had a job to do since they were pretty much out of everything their stock needed to be replenished. Ze was in charge of the potions. It wasn't because she was the best with potions, that would be Tesser or Primalis. She was just the best at haggling. And since potions tended to be the things that were most expensive, that was where she was most needed.

The potion shop they most frequented was in the middle of town with most of the other shops. There were a few shops that sold potions in town, but only one that specialized. After a while, they realized it was best to go to someone who knew exactly what they were doing.

When she opened the door to Pollie's Potion Pavilion, a little bell told the shopkeeper, Pollie, she'd arrived. Pollie was a round woman who looked like she should be out milking cows instead of brewing potions. She was a middle-aged human who had done more with the first half of her life than most people did with all of theirs. Ze liked her because she was always willing to give advice to women about life, even if the woman was three times older than her. It didn't matter to Pollie; everyone needed advice, even if they didn't want it.

Also, if she talked long enough, you'd hear some wild stories about her younger years. It would almost always start off with something along the lines of 'Oh this one time I had to jump out a window in just me shif because his mother and sister came home and I was fucking both of them too.' Since Ze loved hearing stories like that, she never minded going to Pollie's.

The two women sometimes swapped stories about things they'd done. Pollie had a soft spot for Ze and would often give her a discount because of it.

Pollie walked out from her back room to see who had entered her shop. Seeing it was Ze, a large grin spread across her face.

"Oh, my dear, now aren't you a sight for sore eyes. Come here and let me give you a hug," Pollie happily said, opening her arm for Ze. Pollie was one of the few people. Ze felt comfortable hugging. It was always a nice warm hug that made you feel safe.

"How are you doing, Pollie?" Ze asked when they let go of each other.

"Doin' well. Since you're out and about, I take it your bother is doing better?"

"Yes, much better. Completely healed."

"Good to hear, good to hear. I take it you're here on business then?"

"How'd you know?"

"Oh, I just have a feeling about things." Pollie gave her a playful wink.

"Checking out an abandoned dungeon a little bit out of town in the mountains."

"Um, I don't think anyone has been in that thing in a while. It's been there since I've lived here."

That was a good sign. Even if someone had cleaned out all the treasure, there still would be monsters who had found their way into the dungeon. Treasure would be preferred, but they would take what they could get. Such was the life of an adventure.

"Guess it's about time someone checked it out."

"And it might as well be you lot." Pollie let out a laugh.

"Might as well." Ze couldn't help but laugh with her. It was nice to have a conversation without anything else brewing below the surface. At home currently, it was like everyone was walking on eggshells and didn't want to actually talk about anything.

"Let's get well stocked then."

Pollie started taking out various potions she knew Ze would need. They'd been going to her for so long that she just knew what they would need. Any time they came to her, they would just tell her what they were doing, and she'd hand them a crate of potions. Every time it was the same amount. So very little was said during this process since they trusted each other to not check one another.

The actual buying wasn't what took you a long time in Pollie's shop it was the talking, which was a small price to pay for the best potions in town.

It was well past midday when Zo started walking back to the house. Her crate of potions was filled to the brim. Pollie had stuffed straw in between the bottles so they wouldn't break. Even with the straw, the glass bottles clinked together slightly as she walked. Pollie had made sure they were over-prepared, as always.

The afternoon was well spent Pollie had regaled her about a tavern she used to be a barmaid at. She had told her about all the different adventuring parties she had met and all the different things they had been paid in. The weirdest being goblin noses.

"Most people go for the ears, but honestly, you can take any body part to show proof of kill. I just had to take them down to the town leader's house for payment."

Zo couldn't help but smile at Pollie's stories. They were from a life well lived. Even though she know Pollie was in her later years, none of them had ever gotten a real answer about her age. Which only made them want to know more.

The storage room was getting full. It looked like the other had started to bring back the items they'd been tasked with too. Which meant they'd be all ready for tomorrow.

The feeling of being ready was definitely nice. There had been more than enough times where they'd gone off somewhere more than less prepared, to put it lightly. They'd figured it out and gotten out but only just. And it was much better to be safe than sorry. If she could not have a repeat adventure of running for her life, Zo would greatly prefer it.

"It looks like you're getting ready to go somewhere," Quinton's voice said behind her. At this point, she was used to him showing up unannounced most of the time behind her.

She wasn't sure if it was to scare her, to assert dominance over her, or it was just how he was. But considering how he acted towards her during other times, she would guess it was the latter.

"Raiding a dungeon tomorrow. I'll probably be busy for the next week or so," Ze told him as she turned around to face him.

"You are an adventurer, after all. It would be more surprising if you weren't going off to some random dungeon."

"I'm glad you understand." Ze was actually glad he understood there had been way too many people who didn't. If she spent any time with someone who wasn't an adventurer, the conversation always come up about her stopping. Which wasn't something she wanted to do any time soon.

"Are you busy..."

"I'm getting things ready, but I can be persuaded to take a break."

Quinton didn't need any more encouragement. He brush his hand through her hair and then landed on her cheek. It was a gentle touch that felt more intimate than she was expecting. There was nothing wrong with that, but it was a bit of a surprise. Considering they'd spent a few nights cuddling now, she shouldn't be surprised but old habits die hard.

That was the end of his gentleness as he then grabbed a fist full of her hair to pull her neck to the side. Without missing a beat, he attacked the exposed neck with kisses, bites, and licks, which earned him a happy moan from Ze. It was nice to have someone else take control.

She wanted to be man-handled, fae handled? To be completely at his mercy as a plaything. Being in control all the time was tiring. He made her feel like she could lose that control. This surprised her. She wasn't sure if that was a good or bad thing yet. But this was not the time to figure it out.

"I'll let you choose what surface I fuck you on," Quinton

whispered into her ear. It sent a chill down her spine.

Ze quickly took a mental rundown of everything in the study that would survive their activities.

"There's a desk in the corner. It's kinda the perfect height, and I've always wanted to-"

She was cut off by a long hard kiss from Quinton. He then pulled her over to the desk, not so gently. The back of her thighs hit the front of the drawers.

His lips crushed against her again. His hand stilled in her hair, guiding her however he liked. It sent a thrill through her. She was already dripping after just kissing and touching. She felt like a teenager again.

Both were breathing heavily.

Equally excited about their current activities.

Pulling away, Quinton let go of her hair and spun her around. Hooking his fingers on the top of her pants, he shoved them down. His hand ran up her stomach, across her chest, and to her neck, gripping it, bringing a labored breath from Zo's lips. He pulled her closer to him and almost growled in her ear.

"You're already so ready for me. Have you been wanting me since I last saw you?" He asked as his fingers grazed her folds, barely touching her. It only made her wetter, making her shudder against him. All Zo could manage was a gasp. This wasn't good enough for Quinton.

"I asked you a question," he growled again, tightening his grip on her neck. Just enough so she'd feel lightheaded but not enough to actually hurt her.

"Yes, I've thought about you touching me, being with you," Ze managed to gasp.

"And this excites you?"

"Yes"

"Good." it was almost as if he was grateful she was thinking about him. As if he couldn't believe she'd had him on her mind. Or that he wasn't the only one thinking about it.

She heard the rustling of fabric, and Ze could only guess he was also taking off his pants. All while his hand gripped her throat, not wanting to let go.

Feeling his other hand push her back down so she was bent over the desk excited her even more. She could feel how hard and ready he was against her thigh.

Now fully bent over the table. Quinton had moved his hand from the front of her neck to the back. Using his grip to hold her in place. Still applying pressure but in a different way. His other hand spread across her back. It then glided over her to grip her fleshy butt. In no way was Zo out of shape, she had defined muscle from years of adventuring, but boy, did she have an ass. It was something Quintion had noticed the first time he saw her when she came to make a deal. And he was happily grabbing it now.

On full display for him, Zo was waiting and wanting. She didn't know if she could stand to wait for him any longer. She was about to start begging, but any words that were going to be said were instantly cut off by him plunging himself into her.

The trusts were hard and fast. Making her hips bump into the desk, causing it to rock and bump against the wall. Zo was glad she picked something sturdy, not wanting to end up in a pile of debris on the ground. She knew there would be bruises later, but she didn't care. She needed him.

Quinton gripped her neck, pulling her up to him. He repositioned his hand so he was gripping the front again, keeping her in place while he continued to trust. Ze could hear his ragged breathing in her ear and feel it against her neck. He haphazardly put sloppy kisses on her neck and shoulder.

"Fuck you feel amazing." She heard him gasp in between heavy breaths. It was more to himself than to her. But she took to the compliment all the same.

Biting her ear, she could feel him shudder against her. Emptying himself into her. He gave a few more good hard thrusts into her before pulling out and placing a sloppy kiss on her collar. Quinton then gently placed her on the desk before lying next to her.

Both were out of breath neither could help but smile. Zo make sure to position herself so she could look at him. She felt his hand resting on her lower back.

"That was a little rougher than usual. Was that alright?" Quinton asked tentatively once his breath started to return to normal. It was as if he was worried he'd made a mistake.

"It was great. I enjoyed myself. You don't have to worry about being gentle with me. You know I'm not delicate," Ze told him, no longer out of breath but still not ready to move.

"I know that, but I want to ensure we enjoy ourselves. This isn't a one-way street." The hand resting on her gave her a reassuring squeeze.

11

Chapter 11

With all the supplies picked up and the dungeon researched, the team was ready to go. Tesser was the only one not going as he didn't much like the whole adventure part of adventuring. He did do some research on the dungeon for them, though.

It had been first discovered over 150 years ago. A few parties had a record of going through it, but the whole system wasn't mapped, which meant more chance of treasure which was a definite pro. The con about that was there was only half a map, and they didn't know what to expect from the blank spaces. Also, that meant they didn't know how big it was.

Tesser had made them an enchanted map of all the other adventures' maps. With little notes here and there saying this team found this here, but the other team found this. Or they only passed this room but didn't go in. The map would fill in the missing spaces as they came to it giving them a better idea of the whole dungeon. Also once they entered the dungeon, there would be little dots showing where they were in relation to the map.

The six, Ze, Zo, Primalis, Gorran, Sallen, and Wina, set out ready for their first proper adventure in about two months. It was a great feeling getting out of the town and back into the more wild parts of the world. Adventuring was in all their blood. It didn't feel right if they didn't go out to who knows where.

The walk to the dungeon was uneventful. At this point, Ze had come to terms with the fact Zo was going to have a baby with a fae, or at least he was no longer staring daggers at her back. And she didn't feel like she had to walk on eggshells around him.

Primalis still looked between the siblings from time to time making sure they weren't going to burst into a fight. But a general nervousness was very common from her. So there wasn't much of a difference only difference was what her nervousness was about.

Wina kept having to tell Sallen to stop looking at Ze with sad eyes. He was doing his best, but Ze could often feel his eyes on her. Maybe contemplating if he should give pregnancy advice. He was the only one with a kid from the whole party. Mind you it was from a one-night stand and he wasn't there for much of the pregnancy. But he felt like he should try to help as best he could. Being an older brother also helped, and he might have sound advice. Zo just hadn't found out yet.

As far as Zo knew someone had told Gorran but he hadn't brought it up to her yet. If no one had told him it wasn't a huge deal, but at the rate, she and Quinton were going she was going to be pregnant soon. Gorran was a sweetheart even if he wasn't the smartest person around. He always had his friend's best interests in mind.

Once they got to the dungeon's entrance, they decided to camp out for the night. It would be better to go in fully rested instead of after they'd walked all day.

CHAPTER 11

The last time Zo was awakened by the sound of the forest around her was when she had gone to make a deal with Quinton. Even though it had only been a few weeks, it felt like a lifetime ago. She didn't like the idea of having an empty bed for the next few days or weeks. But she knew it would mean their reunion would be even better when it happened.

She unconsciously touched her breast where his mark was. She knew he was watching. Instead of it being creepy, it was a nice reminder that he was close by if she needed him.

After looking around, she noticed the only one up was Gorran. He'd started a fire and looked like he was making breakfast for everyone. Zo made her way over to him. Taking a seat by the fire he'd made.

"Morning Zo, I caught some rabbit. It should be done in a bit," Gorran said. His voice was deep but slightly scary, but his tone was light and welcoming.

"Sounds great, thanks," Zo replied, getting comfortable.

There was silence between them for a bit as the meat cooked over the campfire.

"Ze told me what's happening," He said after a bit.

He raised a hand to stop Zo from saying anything.

"You have a way of always knowing what's right for you. It sounds like it was your decision, and it saved Ze. I'll trust you and support you how you need me to."

Zo was shocked. Gorran wasn't the most well-spoken person, but when he was, it was gems like this. It was a nice feeling to have your friend there to back you up. Especially since everyone else told her how much they disagreed with her decision. She didn't know if Gorran agreed or disagreed it wasn't important, so he didn't tell her.

"Thank you," Was all Ze said, and it was all that needed to be said.

They sat in silence, eating and waiting for the others to wake up. It wasn't an uncomfortable silence, and it was the first time in the last few weeks Zo didn't feel like she was waiting for someone to say something to her, but they didn't want to because they knew it would upset her. She felt relaxed. It was good to have that feeling back.

Primalis was the next one up, but she was anything but awake. She was anything but a morning person. She flopped next to the fire and pulled out a little glass vile of her morning potion that woke her up. Zo didn't think it did anything, but Primalis swore by it. She slowly started to become more awake, nibbling on some rabbit.

Wina waved good morning to them as she goes off to do her morning prayers. She needed a quiet place to do it, and the rest of the party respected that. None of them would talk to her till she started the conversation so that she could do what she needed.

After waving good morning to Wina as she went to go meditate, Sallen settled in between Gorran and Primalis. For a reason that no one could understand or figure out, he was always in a chipper mood. He was a morning, day, and night person. There had been more than a few times he was out all night at a tavern or pub and then was up and about at the crack of dawn, ready to work. The working theory was he'd made an unholy deal of some kind. No one knew with who or what. And no one wanted to ask because they really didn't want to know.

Sallen took his portion of the rabbit as he said good morning to everyone else around the fire. It was a nice morning. It reminded Zo of all the times before Ze got sick. It felt normal. It was nice to feel normal again. She hoped everything would go back to normal soon. She really missed normal. So far, it was slowly inching back toward that. If only Ze hadn't walked in on her and Quinton, maybe they could get there someday.

Ze normally was the last to wake up. Zo had noted that he and Primalis had slept close to each other last night and a bit away from everyone else. If things had been better between her and her twin, Zo would have teased him about it. She still wasn't sure how she felt about him getting close to Primalis. She hated that she was opposed to it. She should be happy for them.

But it was hard and made her understand how Ze felt slightly. It was hard not to see it as Primalis was taking Ze away from her. But, in reality, they had already started to drift apart. Not in a bad way but because they no longer only rely on each other to survive. They had a makeshift new family they knew would be there for them if needed. In whatever shape or form they needed them. Just as the twins would be there for them.

Ze finally joined them by the fire sliding in by Primalis. She handed him some rabbit to help him wake up. She offered him some of her position, but he shook his head. Even if he thought she was cute and liked her, he still couldn't be persuaded to try her connotation.

"Ah, good, everyone is up," Wina said, joining them "are you just waiting for me?"

"Rabbit?" Gorran asked, holding out the last position to her.

"Thanks."

"We should pack up and head in. Who knows what awaits us down there," Zo said, standing up and dusting off her pants. There was a murmur of agreement as they all got up to get ready to go into the dungeon. Wina quickly finished her breakfast, joining the rest of the party.

12

Chapter 12

The entrance of the dungeon was covered by vines and well off the beaten path. It was a surprise that Tesser and Gorran were able to find it at all.

"How were you able to find this place?" Ze asked as they started their descent into the cave.

"We stopped by it on our way back. Tesser felt some magic or something sorcerery," Gorran told them.

"Which must have been the reason he wanted us to check it out," Wina said.

They quietly descended into the dungeon, all on alert. Even if a dungeon was old you never knew what you were going to find in one. Monsters and creatures often used them as homes or nests. One wrong noise and they all would be in the middle of a fight without any warning.

Wina was in charge of the magical map that Tesser had made them. She quietly gave directions. They wanted to check out some of the unmapped areas of the dungeon. They had a higher chance of reward.

When a turned a corner, the path was covered in vines. From

what they could tell, it was more than just a plant. Ze tapped it slightly with his toe to see if it would move. When there was no movement, Sallen started to walk down the hallway only to be stopped by Zo.

She grabbed a small stone from the ground and throw it into the hallway, making sure to hit as many vines as possible. That's when everything started moving.

The vines whipped back and forth violently, and a snarl was heard from somewhere within the mess of vines.

"Wina or Primals, you think you could give us some fire?" Zo asked.

"To completely fry it, both of us should do it," Primalis said, looking at Wina, who nodded in agreement.

The two women stepped in front of the group and drew from their respective magics within themselves. Then flames shot out of their hands, filling the hallway.

The others shielded their faces from the heat. A high-pitched scream could be heard from the heart of the tangle of vines. The vines thrashed back and forth, trying to get to Wina and Primals. Luckily their flames were too intense, and there was no danger to them or the rest of the party. The vines finally stopped moving a small whine was let out by the sentient plant.

"We should be good to get through," Wina said to the rest of the group.

They made their way through the burnt vines to a large room that hadn't been on the map. At first glance, it didn't look like anything was there, just a large empty stone room. But all of them knew appearances were deceiving. The group fanned out to search the room.

Zo ran her hands over the stone walls looking for anything that was out of place, no matter how small or insignificant feeling. Ze looked at one of the pillars in the middle of the room. Wina looked for any magical elements or items within the room. Sallen started poking at the stone flooring to see if there was anything out of place. Gorran Started looking at the ceiling to see if there was anything of interest there. Primalis used her magic to look for any traps.

For a while, they were all quiet each looking around the room to see if there was anything there. It wouldn't be unheard of to have an empty room that leads nowhere in a dungeon, but it was still not overly normal. It usually meant there was something hidden in it or a trap ready to spring at any moment. All of them were thinking the same thing, making sure to be on guard. The last thing they wanted was to have to figure out how to get out of a trap.

Of course, since all of them were thinking about a trap and worried about it, it was inevitable that something would happen.

"Oh shit," Ze said as his hand pushed in a brick on one of the pillars. Everyone heard him and instantly stopped. They all looked around, trying to figure out what was about to happen.

That was when the giant slab of rock slid down, blocking the stairway they took to get down there.

"Fuck, Gorran, do you think you can break throw?" Zo asked as they ran up to the stone slab.

"I'll definitely try," He said as he swung his giant hammer. Before he could hit anything, though, the floor underneath them dropped out, causing all of them to slide down a shoot.

They all were diverted down different slides. Splitting them up.

Zo was deposited in a tunnel. The walls were hard-packed dirt that looked like they had been scarped away by some sort of creature. Whatever it was, she hoped it was long gone now. The tunnel wasn't large, so she had to crawl on her hands and knees to move around it. The slide had deposited her at the end of the tunnel, and there was only one way to go.

Without anywhere else to go or anything else she could do, Zo started crawling in the only direction that was available. Being half-elf meant she had a better vision in dark places but even with better vision, it was hard to see. No sunlight reached down this far, and there were no torches here either. All she could do was keep moving forward.

There was no way to track time in the tunnel, so Zo didn't know how long she had been crawling, but it felt like a while. So when it was finally starting to get lighter, she had to let out a sigh of relief. Being stuck in a tunnel, not knowing where it was taking her, had been a stress she had not wanted at all today.

As the light got brighter, it made her crawl faster. You never know how much you miss the light until you don't have it. Finally, Zo reached the end of the tunnel. It emptied into a large round room carved out of the same hard dirt the tunnel was carved out of. That didn't put her at ease. She just hoped whatever had made the tunnel and this room was no longer here.

The light that she was following came from some mushrooms that were fluorescent. Zo walked over to one and pulled it off the wall, hoping it wouldn't stop glowing when she picked it up. Luckily it didn't. She breathed a sigh of relief.

"Hello? Anyone there? Can anyone hear me?" She called into the open room, hoping one of the other members of her party would be able to hear her. The only thing that answered her was her echo. There was no way to talk to each other; the best they had was paper they could talk to Tesser.

You would write something on it then it would appear on a matching one he had. Once he replied, it would appear on your paper. It was great for getting information when they were on an adventure but wouldn't help Zo in this situation.

Zo couldn't help but let out a sigh. She'd made it out of the tunnel, but she was now alone in what looked like used to be a den of some sort. She really hoped the den part was in the past tense. She did not want to fight whatever carved it by herself.

The only thing she could do was move forward, so she did. With her mushroom in hand, she started making her way toward the other side of the den. That's when she started to hear movement.

Taking any monster on by yourself was stupid, even if it was a small monster. Hunting was one thing, but that was for survival. This was also about survival. If you hear a monster and you're alone, you run.

Cautiously Zo walked toward what she thought would be the exit. She kept looking back and forth, listening to any more movement.

That's when she saw it. The long legs of a giant poison spider moved in and out of her field of vision.

Not good.

She needed to get out of here now. It may not be the thing that made these tunnels, but it definitely lived here now. And Zo did not want to find out just how big it had gotten down here. She made a break for an opening that looked like it would be too small for the spider to get through. Also, the vegetation was more than just the mushrooms, which meant it probably lead somewhere. At least, that was what she was hoping for.

She was about to make it when the spider sprayed webbing in front of her, blocking the path. She would have to cut, throw or burn the webs in order to get out, but that was something she didn't have time for. Not while she was about to become this spider's next meal.

As quick as ever, Zo instantly drops her mushroom light and lets loose two arrows at the same time. Hitting the spider in the middle of the face.

The spider lets out a painful screech and darts toward Zo. She dives out of the way, dodging the first attack. But she knows she won't be able to keep this up for long. She shoots another arrow, this time only gracing the creature.

This was bad. She was alone with a giant poison spider, and her exit was blocked. The only other thing she would be able to do was hit one of the tunnels and hope the spider's legs wouldn't be able to grab her. Or its poison spray wouldn't get her. Or the webs. She didn't like any of those options.

The will to live was strong, though, and giving up was not an option. Zo Darted for the closest tunnel knowing it would at least buy her some time. She was almost there then she felt it. Webs wrapped around her, pulling her back.

It got her.

She was done.

This was how she died. Via spider. Not how she'd imagined herself dying, but most people don't like thinking about it. For adventures, it was a fact of life. Sometimes you go on adventures, and you don't come back. Zo just never thought it'd be like this alone in a cave.

That was when she realized she wasn't alone.

"Quinton, help."

13

Chapter 13

The giant spider crawled closer as Zo tried to pull herself out of the sticky webs. But the more she struggled, the more tangled she became. For the first time in a long time, she was scared.

Now over her baring, its fangs, the spider prepared to dive in. She closed her eyes, not wanting to look at the creature as it started eating her.

But the pain never came.

Echoing through the cavern were the spider's screeches of pain. Zo opened her eyes to see Quinton standing over her. The black mist that had been around him when she first met was now filling the room. Also, the mask he had been wearing covered his face.

"This will only take a moment. Please don't try to move," Quinton's voice is low and angry. It's nothing like his normal unamused tone or his playful, flirting voice. Zo can do nothing but obey.

Quinton darted toward the spider and ripped off one of its legs. Sending black blood spraying all over the room. He made quick work of the rest of its legs. The spider no longer could support itself.

Its leg stubs failed at trying to move its large body. The screeching has only gotten louder the more injured the spider became as Quinton got closer to its face. The spider tried to bite him, only to have its fangs ripped out.

The screeching instantly stopped as Quinton ripped the spider's head off. Leaving it to pool black blood in the middle of the floor.

Quinton walked back towards Zo. As he did the mist dissipated. She wondered if it had to do with his mood. Because it never was there when they were alone together. He then pulled off his mask for that to disappear into mist as well.

He crouched down next to Zo and gently caressed her cheek. She let out a sigh of relief, knowing that she was safe. He brought calm and comfort to her. The webs had now completely covered her at this point and made it so she couldn't talk. She mumbled something along the lines of 'I'm so glad you're here'

"I'm going to have to cut this off you. Hold still," He told her, pulling a small blade out from nowhere.

Zo just nodded, watching him work. He cut her out of the webs carefully. Making sure not to nick her skin. She was already bruised and scraped up from the falling and crawling earlier. But luckily the spider hadn't had time to poison her.

Pulling away the rest of the webs, Quinton was able to free her. The second she was free, Zo wrapped her arms around him. He eagerly returned the hug pulling her tighter. He took the moment to just breathe her in remembering her sent and enjoying just benign there.

"I'm glad you're alright," Quiton said into her neck. It was almost a whisper more to himself than to her.

"For a moment, there I wasn't. Thank you," Zo responded,

pulling him even tighter. She didn't want to let go out of fear he wasn't real.

All Quinton could do was hold her. He was glad to have her in his arms again. Especially since she called him into a spider's den, he knew adventuring was dangerous, but it hadn't really crossed his mind that he'd lose her. Zo was strong and smart. She wasn't going to die adventuring. That was when it hit him. He didn't want to lose her.

Ever. Period

Taking care of the spider was easy enough, but what if there was something else he couldn't take care of? What if he'd gotten her a few seconds later?

Quinton squeezed Zo harder. She hadn't let go of him even though she'd confirmed he was real at this point.

"Why are you alone," Quinton finally asked. Another reason he hadn't been worried was that she was heading out with a large party. People she trusted and was used to working with.

"We got separated by a trap. I'm not sure where anyone else is," Zo told him, keeping a firm grip on him.

The last thing she'd thought before she called for him was, 'I need to survive so I can see Quinton again'. It had surprised her for sure. But she knew she wanted him in her life. Needed him in her life.

"I'm just glad you're alright. I don't want to lose you."

Was that concern she heard in his voice? Was he worried about her? No, it must be that he'd have to make another deal if she couldn't fill her end of it. If she died without fulfilling her end of the deal, what would happen to Ze?

"Well, lucky for you, you don't have to find another person to make a deal with. I'm still able to deliver that baby to you." She said it as a joke but needed to know if that was all she was to him. So she could get this done, push down her feelings, and move on.

Zo feels Quinton visibly stiffen. It's as if he's been struck by something. In a sense, he was. His mind reeled at the idea that that was all she saw their relationship as. A deal she needed to fill. If that was the case, was he better off just leaving it at that? But something inside him told him to tell her otherwise.

"Our meeting may not have been ideal, Zo, but I'm glad it happened. And I can't think of a place I'd rather be than by your side," the words came out of his mouth before he could really think. Good bad he didn't know, but it was out there now.

After what felt like an eternity, Zo just looked at Quinton. She didn't believe what he just said. He wanted to be with her. He liked being by her side.

"What does that mean?" Was all she could say.

"What do you mean 'what does that mean'?!"

"I mean, you want to be by my side, but in what context? Does that mean you care about me? But in what context? Do you feel the same way about me as I do about you?"

"Zo, it means I love you that I fell in love with you. That I don't want to lose you. That I want to be with you."

This made her freeze. Did she love him? She liked being by him and wanted to wake up to him every morning. She thought about him when he wasn't there. But did that mean Zo was in love with him? All she knew was she wanted to be with him. She cared about him, and saying he loved her made her very happy.

The only sensible answer was to crush her lips against his.

He nipped at her bottom lip, asking for entrance. Which she happily allowed. His tongue ran over her lips and stroked hers. It was the most passionate they'd ever been, and they couldn't get enough of each other.

Zo pulled away.

"I don't know if I'm ready to say it back, but even if you wanted to, I don't think I would be able to let you go," She told him, holding his face close to hers.

Quinton then picked her up bridal style. Zo was anything but a princess or a damsel in distress, but for him, she'd pretend.

"Let's get you out of this dungeon first, though," He said, kissing her as he teleported both of them outside the entrance.

14

Chapter 14

"ZO!"

Zo and Quinton both swiveled their heads toward the yell. The rest of her party all were running toward her. They'd been sitting in a circle preparing for what looked like a battle. When the initial shock of seeing Zo safe and alive had worn off they realized that Quinton was holding her in his arms.

"You!" Ze yelled loudly pointing at Quinton "Were you the reason we got separated?"

"Contrary to your insistent belief I do actually care about your sister's well-being. And she would have been a lot safer staying with your group than alone down in the dungeon," Quinton retorted.

Zo just rolled her eyes and was not in the mood to be literally in the middle of an argument between Ze and Quinton right now. The two men seemed determined not to like each other. Quinton's grip on her tighten as if he was worried she'd leave his arms and go to her brother. But her mind was made up he was going to be in her life, and Ze would just have to get used to it.

"Both of you, stop it! Ze, Quin was the one who saved me, not the one who separated us. That was a trap in the dungeon. It happens. Quin, Ze is not your enemy, both of you stop acting like you are. And finally, what were you guys doing? It looks like you're ready for war?"

"We were getting ready to come get you," Wina said holding a mace about the same size as her.

"After we all found each other and couldn't find you, we used the map to get back to the surface and then were going to resupply and go get you," Primalis told her.

"I'm so glad you're alright," Gorran added.

"I just have one question," Sullan started "Who's this?"

He pointed to Quinton. Everyone else's eyes went right to the fae now all with the same question.

"It's the fae!" Ze told them all. He said it in a way as if it was obvious who Quinton was. Everyone turned to look at Ze, then turned back to look at Quinton. Finally, their eyes landed on Zo, still gripped in Quinton's arms.

"I get it now," Wina said after giving Quinton a once over.

"Completely," Primalis agreed. Gorran and Sullan just nodded in agreement. Ze looked between Quinton and his friends in disbelief.

Zo couldn't help a blush coming on. Making the tips of her pointed ears turn bright red.

"Alright, ok. Yes, this is the fae that healed Ze because I made a deal with him. I'm alright if we could all just talk about something else," Zo said holding her hands up. She wasn't used to being the center of attention or feeling so helpless. But it didn't look like Quinton was going to let her go any time soon.

"Well, we've found you're party. They have seen you're completely fine. We'll be going then. We'll see you back at home," Quinton said before he teleported them again.

The rest of the party could make out Zo's argument as they vanished into the back mist.

"He's so annoying," Ze yelled after they disappeared. Causing the rest of the group to laugh.

Her room faded into view as the black mist cleared up. It was surprisingly warm. Zo had always imagined Quinton's mist was like normal mist but somehow colder. It was a nice feeling almost as if a warm cloud warped you in a blanket.

Quinton walked over to her bed and sat down, still carrying her. He then toed off his boots with a little difficulty and set her down on his lap. So his hands could be free to take off her boots. After both their boots were off, he took off her traveling cloak and unstrapped her weapons and travel pouches. When he was done stripping her down to just her top and pants, Quinton moved on to himself. Taking off his jacket and vest. Neither of them talked while he did this. Normally Zo would have moved out of his grasp as soon as he let go, but she stayed on his lap not wanting to move.

When he was done taking off his clothes, he wrapped his arms around her waist and fell back onto the bed, taking her with him. They just moved to adjust themselves, getting comfortable on the bed and in each other's arms.

That's how they stayed till they both dosed off. Falling asleep in each other's arms was a comfort for both of them. Neither wanted to sleep alone again. Especially after they admitted their feelings.

Zo was the first one to wake. She wasn't sure how long they stayed like that in each other's arms, but it left her with a smile on her face. Quinton looked so peaceful lying next to her. His arm was still draped around her waist. When she moved, he responded by pulling her closer to him. Zo responded by kissing his forehead.

His eyes opened slightly and was welcomed to the sight of Zo's face laying next to him. She had a soft smile that matched his.

Without warning, he pulled her to him crushing their lips together. He needed her. He needed her now. Once their lips met it was like a fire went through both of them.

Zo pulled at his clothes. There were way too many layers in between them. She wanted to feel his skin on hers. They had no regard for how they got the clothes off or where they landed they just knew that they need to come off. Now.

In a flurry of hands kisses and a few frustrated noises, they were both now fully naked. Quinton dove in, attacking first her neck, and then he moved down her chest. He made sure to kiss his mark on the way down to her breast. When he did even more heat ran through Zo, it was as if he just reaffirmed his love for her.

He took one nipple in his mouth and the other he rolled between his fingers. Zo ran her hands through his hair. Sucking in air as he started to suck on her nipple. He then lightly bit it, causing a gasp from her. She gripped his hair, pulling it slightly.

"You want more?" He asked, kissing around the bite mark. Zo nodded eagerly.

"I can't hear you. You're going to have to use your words," Quinton told her with a playful tone to his voice. The sound of it sent a shock through her. At that moment, she knew if he used that voice on her, she'd do anything for him. Not because she had to but because she wanted to.

His normal voice almost always sounded bored or like you

weren't worth talking to. But this, she had his full attention, and she never knew how much she craved someone's full undivided attention.

"I want more," Zo was able to force out between heavy breaths.

"Good girl," Quinton told her right before biting down again. While biting on her left nipple, he rolled the other one in between his fingers.

Zo couldn't help but buck her hips up towards him. This just caused him to let out a small laugh.

"Such a needy girl," was all he said. He met her thrusts so she had something to grind against. And to see what effect she was having on him. He was completely hard and so close to her folds. Zo let out a whimper.

She tried to move so he could slide into her or at least so she could grind against his already hard length.

"I need you," she moaned, moving her body to be as close to him as possible.

Quinton stopped biting her nipple, which made Zo give a small, sad whimper. But it only lasted a second as he trailed kisses back up her neck. Cupping her cheek, he pulled her into a hard kiss. His hand found its way into her hair, pulling her towards him. They both felt like they couldn't be close enough to each other.

"I need you too," He said, pulling away for a second. It was quick and quiet but enough. But at that moment, the only other thing that mattered to Zo was Quinton. Anything he said or did, no matter how quiet or small, she would know.

Before entering her, he rubbed his head against her folds. Both teasing her and making sure she was ready for him. There was no question she was ready. His tip easily ran up and down her folds. From top to bottom. Causing her to moan and squirm under him.

Not wanting to make her wait anymore, Quinton pushed himself inside her. She was tight, warm, and sopping wet. Pulling a groan of pleasure out of him as he entered her.

Even though they'd had sex multiple times now, this time felt different. This time they felt different. This wasn't just a quick lay or a mark off a checklist for a quest. They both wanted this to be here in each other's arms, as close as two people could physically be. There was no going back after this.

Never losing eye contact, Quinton started to move. He was slow at first, enjoying the feeling of her. Zo clung to him like a life raft, never wanting to let go. Then as if on cue, he started speeding up.

Faster, harder, their eyes never leaving each other.

As if timed, they both felt the building pressure. Zo's nails dug into Quinton's back, and his fingers left bruises on her shoulders. At the moment they both came everything was right.

They both were at peace, falling asleep in each other's arms.

15

Chapter 15

It was Quinton who woke up first. The first thing he saw when he opened his eyes was Zo. She was still asleep, and her expression could only be described as content. Quinton couldn't help himself as he lightly kissed her forehead. It felt right to wake up next to her and then give her affection. He wouldn't mind if this was the start of his days from now on.

He felt her wake up as soon as he kissed her. He felt a little bad for waking her, but also it meant he could talk to her, which he found himself looking forward to. Zo smiled as soon as she opened her eyes.

Her first thought was how happy she was to wake up next to Quinton. She never really thought about who her long-term partner would be. Forever always seemed like a pipe dream. Something that happened to other people but not to her. Yet here she was in bed and in the arms of a man she was willing to try with.

"Good morning," Quinton said with a smile matching hers.

"Morning," She replied, snuggling into him.

"How'd you sleep?"

"Good, all thanks to you."

"Are you calling me a sleep aid now?"

"And other things."

Zo couldn't help herself from smiling more. She playfully tapped his cheek with her finger as she talked. Her taps became a soft caress. Quinton's face softened, and he leaned into her hand. Then he leaned into a kiss.

This was how he wanted to wake up from now on. There was no other way he wanted it.

"What are these other things I am good at?" He asked once he pulled away from their kiss.

"I do believe that list is long, and you checked many of those things off last night."

"I wouldn't mind checking off more things this morning."

Zo just smiled and kissed him again. As much as she wanted to fall into his arms and enjoy another round of amazing sex, there was one thing still at the back of her mind.

She pulled away from him and propped herself up on her arm.

"Quin, about our deal," She started.

"Yes?" He asked, unsure where she was going with this line of questioning.

"I'm supposed to give you my firstborn."

"Yes, which you made sure was going to be mine. Because you're a sneaky smart woman."

"I might be, but what does that mean?"

"I thought you understood the process, but if you need more explanation, I can give you a hands-on demonstration."

"No, I mean when our deal had been filled. And I give you my firstborn. What happens then?"

"We raise it. I mean, it is a baby. It can't do anything on its own."

"So you're staying?"

"Did you not want me to?"

Zo grabbed him and pulled him into a crushing kiss. She never wanted him to leave. For the rest of her life, she wanted him here. The idea of them together with their child was something she never realized she wanted. And now she couldn't think of anything else she wanted more.

"You said you'd stay by my side. That better include raising our child together," She told him once she pulled away from their kiss.

"Our deal was to have a child together. It never said anything about me leaving."

"Then we should get on finalizing that deal. I don't want to keep you waiting.

About the Author

When Vebecca isn't being a hopeless romantic she spends her time annoying her husband. They live in California together with way to many house plants and even more books and VHSs.

www.ingramcontent.com/pod-product-compliance
Lightning Source LLC
LaVergne TN
LVHW090533110826
845146LV00003B/1080

* 9 7 9 8 9 8 8 4 9 6 6 1 8 *